Praise fo

'Chris Flynn has written a brilliant, hilarious and curiously moving novel, featuring one of the best narrators in literary history and – without a doubt – the single best narrator in natural history. I simply love this story.' **Elizabeth Gilbert**

'*Mammoth* is astonishing, a novel that is by turns playful, uncomfortably excoriating, very funny and always deeply humane. The voice in *Mammoth* doesn't sound like a voice I've ever heard before and for those of us who love books and reading this is the pleasure and the hope that we are always chasing. This novel delivers. It is both a requiem for lost worlds and lost time, and it is also a sheer joy.' **Christos Tsiolkas**

'*Mammoth* is an extraordinary gambit of the storytelling imagination of Chris Flynn, and a new way of listening to all the narratives of what we have supplanted. *Mammoth* is playful and serious, encapsulating the macro-history of all life in the tale of one species.' **Tom Keneally**

'If you've been feeling like the novel is an endangered species, then *Mammoth* is the book to bring it back to life. *Mammoth* shows anthropocentrism as the laughable delusion that it is, while still affirming the value and significance of story. This 13,000-year-old skeleton is my favourite character in years, and this hilarious and heartbreaking book is precisely what we hominids need right now.' **Emily Bitto**

'Funny, warm and totally unique – I loved it.' **Favel Parrett**

'*Mammoth* looks at humanity's impact on the planet through the eyes of a creature we once shared it with. The real treat is the voice of the central character – curmudgeonly and erudite yet heartbreakingly lost and confused, and utterly believable as a relic of a lost world.' **Meg Keneally**

'Chris Flynn's riveting mixture of fact and whimsy makes previously foreign names like *Palaeospheniscus* and *Canis dirus* memorable fellow travellers like Huck Finn and Ulysses. He gracefully leverages history to help us think about the future, big pictures and deep time.' **Dr George Church, Professor of Genetics, Harvard Medical School, and head of the Harvard Woolly Mammoth Revival team**

'If a fossil could speak, it would tell a thousand words. Chris Flynn's *Mammoth* elegantly fuses fiction with fact and reminds us that fossils are not just objects of curiosity and fascination. They are the remains of once-living creatures who had emotions, who fought, loved and survived. Flynn brings these extraordinary creatures back to life, from death to décor, through superb storytelling.' **Dr Gilbert Price, Senior Lecturer in Palaeontology, The University of Queensland**

Chris Flynn is the author of *The Glass Kingdom* and *A Tiger in Eden*, which was shortlisted for the Commonwealth Book Prize. His fiction and non-fiction have appeared in *The Age, The Australian, Griffith Review, Meanjin, Australian Book Review, The Saturday Paper, Smith Journal, The Big Issue, Monster Children, McSweeney's* and many other publications. He has conducted interviews for *The Paris Review* and is a regular presenter at literary festivals across Australia. Chris lives on Phillip Island, next to a penguin sanctuary.

chriseflynn.com
@flythefalcon

Book club notes are available at www.uqp.com.au

MAMMOTH

CHRIS FLYNN

UQP

First published 2020 by University of Queensland Press
PO Box 6042, St Lucia, Queensland 4067 Australia

uqp.com.au
uqp@uqp.uq.edu.au

Cover design and illustration by WBYK
Illustrations by Eirian Chapman
Author photograph by Jo Duck
Typeset in 12/18 pt Sina Nova by Post Pre-press Group, Brisbane
Printed in Australia by McPherson's Printing Group

The University of Queensland Press is
assisted by the Australian Government
through the Australia Council, its arts
funding and advisory body.

A catalogue record for this book is available from the National Library of Australia

ISBN 978 0 7022 6274 6 (pbk)
ISBN 978 0 7022 6392 7 (epdf)
ISBN 978 0 7022 6393 4 (epub)
ISBN 978 0 7022 6394 1 (kindle)

University of Queensland Press uses papers that are natural, renewable and
recyclable products made from wood grown in well-managed forests. The logging
and manufacturing processes conform to the environmental regulations of the
country of origin.

Washington Dec. 14. 1800.

Dear Sir,

Your former communications on the subject of the steam engine, I took the liberty of laying before the American Philosophical society, by whom they will be printed in their volume of the present year.

I have heard of the discovery of some large bones, supposed to be of the Mammoth, at about 30. or 40 miles distance from you: and among the bones found, are said to be some which we have never yet been able to procure.

The 1st interesting question is whether they be the bones of the Mammoth? The 2nd what are the particular bones, and could I possibly procure them?

The bones I am most anxious to obtain are those of the head & feet, which are said to be among those found in your state, as also the ossa innominata, and the scapula. Others would also be interesting, though similar ones may be possessed, because they would shew by their similarity that the set belongs to the Mammoth.

Could I so far venture to trouble you on this subject as to engage some of your friends near the place to procure for me the bones above mentioned?

If they are to be bought, I will gladly pay for them whatever you shall agree to as reasonable; and will place the money in N. York as instantaneously after it is made known to me as the post can carry it, as I will all expenses of package, transportation &c. to New York and Philadelphia, where they may be addressed to John Barnes, whose agent (he not being on the spot) will take care of them for me.

Accept assurances of cordial esteem & respect, & my friendly salutations.

Th: Jefferson

Natural History Auction
Fifth Avenue & 29th Street
Manhattan, New York
24 March 2007

The passage of time is difficult for me to parse. I know only that day follows night and then the sun goes down and the cycle begins again. Thirteen thousand, three hundred and fifty-four years is too great an amount of time to comprehend, and yet that is what I am led to believe has elapsed since the antediluvian days. The primeval struggle for survival. Man versus beast. Those were heady times.

We lost, of course. But we gave you a run for your money.

The first time I killed a man – that was a good feeling. Clovis, you were back then. You hunted in packs, just like *Smilodon*, and you were much weaker, but somehow also stronger, more resourceful. Clovis did not roam the grasslands. You stayed in one place. A group might live in a cave, or a basic settlement constructed from hewn trees. You worked marvels with your awkward hands, cleaving and building. Making things. Tools and weapons. Representations of beasts you blithely harvested, carved from the severed horn of a *Coelodonta antiquitatis*, or from the tusk of my dead sister. Remember? The one you speared.

I hated you. We all did. *Glyptodon, Megalonyx, Arctodus, Camelops, Bison priscus, Equus* – all were hunted without mercy. You ate our flesh and wore our hides. You used our bones to fashion ever more complex butchery devices. You burnt the grasslands and forests. You starved us. You drove us to our deaths over cliffs. You hurled rocks and dug pits.

We fought back, but victories were rare. There were too many of you. You were as countless as the stars.

The taking of a life – even that of a pitiless biped – is no small thing. But it made me proud, at the time. You had plenty of bodies to spare. You wouldn't miss one of your hunters.

Every one of us that fell was a disaster. A repository of wisdom and ancestral memory stretching back tens of thousands of your so-called years. It is true what you say, after all. We do not forget. We cannot. When one of us dies, the experiences of thousands disappear with them. Our bloodlines carry more than a blueprint for tusk and trunk. They are replete with the history of family. To kill a mammoth is to kill its primogenitors. One piercing spear can destroy a lineage. This is why the arrival of Clovis in our lands was such an affront. You were bent on not just killing us for pelts to keep you warm in winter and for meat to feed your young, but on erasing us from the world. We knew that if we did nothing it would soon be as if we never existed at all. Our bones would sink into the tar. We would be forgotten.

You tried to ambush me where the canyon narrowed. You thought I didn't know you were up there, that I could not see the trickling pebbles that your strange feet dislodged. Also, I could smell you. Hygiene was never your strong suit.

I had walked that way hundreds of times and, just like my forebears, had rubbed my flanks against the rocky outcrop. Our kind had been doing this for so long that the stone was polished smooth, reflective as water. It was an excellent means of removing ticks and having oneself a good scratch.

I knew something Clovis did not. Those crags further up may have offered prime concealment, but they were unstable. Deep memory told me of how the mountain had collapsed when the earth shook. How it might do so again under similar pressures.

I threw my considerable bulk against the canyon wall. The loose stone crumbled beneath your bony feet. Boulders fell, and men with them. Those of you who were uninjured ran. One of you had an arm pinned under the fallen rocks. Your frantic attempt to push a boulder off the crushed limb was in vain. Your bloodied feet scrabbled in the dirt. It must have been frustrating, being trapped. Terrifying, perhaps, as I bore down on you.

You fell silent as I stood astride you. Choking dust swirled in the air. You closed your eyes and played dead. I leant down and nudged your body with my tusk. You opened your eyes again and squealed in pain. I knew if I pushed hard enough your arm would tear away at the shoulder. I considered doing that, but I am not like man. I do not torture for pleasure.

Your free hand slapped at the ground. You were attempting

to reach a stone knife that had fallen out of reach. Still had some fight in you, despite the odds. I admired that a little. Clovis was tougher than they looked. They clung to life with the ferocity of a cave bear protecting her cubs.

I made it quick. I placed a foot on your chest and pressed down until your sternum cracked and your heart was crushed. Your eyes went wide, and you spat blood over my leg. You expired in a moan of relief.

I wiped your entrails off my foot. One less *Homo sapiens*. The world was a better place.

Who are you talking to, *Mammut*?

That biped. The one with the glasses. I thought perhaps he could hear me, the way he was cocking his head.

None of them can hear you. Believe me, I've tried. And I've been around a lot longer than you, my furry friend. How old did you say you were? Thirteen and a half thousand?

It's been thirteen thousand, three hundred and fifty-four years since I died, in hominid years.

Amateur. Try sixty-seven million.

That cannot be possible. How are there any of your majestic bones left, great lizard?

Good genes, I guess. Avoidance of stress. The excessively dry climate of the Gobi Desert.

I thought you hailed from Florida.

The dealer's from Florida. He claims I'm from China, but it's not true. I was smuggled out of Mongolia. He's going to cop hell when they find out.

How does one go about smuggling the skull of a *Tyrannosaurus rex*?

Actually, I'm a *Tyrannosaurus bataar*. Some hominids call me *Tarbosaurus* but I hate that name, it sucks. We're distant relatives to *Tyrannosaurus rex*. Same basic deal. Go where you like, eat anything that moves. Die in a fight with a young bull or burn to death in lava.

Which was it?

Bit of both. Injured after a scrap, lay down to sleep, couldn't get back up again when the forest was on fire. How'd you check out, *Mammut*?

It's a long story.

We only have until tomorrow. After that, we'll be hanging in the den of some rich guy with a Jurassic Park fantasy. Still, beats spending sixty-seven million years in the desert.

When were you exhumed, *Tyrannosaurus bataar*?

Call me *T. bataar*, dude. Or *T. bat*. Or just *T*. Ninety-one, it was.

In 1991? So you've seen only sixteen years of hominid activity. Well, I have that on you, at least. They brought me up in 1801.

Full skull? Tusks and everything?

No, they had to piece me together. Things were a little hazy for a while but then, to my surprise, here I was. Back again.

It's a bit of a shock, for sure. I kept doing phantom lunges when humans walked past. I never got to taste one. If I were back to my old self, I'd bust us right out of here, friendo. We could go on a rampage in Times Square. Eat us a bunch of tourists and Captain America impersonators.

I'm an herbivore.

No shit? Bummer.

You'd probably try to eat me, *T. bataar*.

I don't know, buddy. Those tusks look pretty fierce. So, 1801, huh? You must have some stories.

Sounds like you're interested in hearing them.

You bet I am.

Careful what you wish for, *T. bataar*.

Look, I'll tell you what. I'll cancel all my appointments and inform my assistant to hold my calls. Impart your wisdom upon me, O great *Mammut* of the steppe.

No need to get sarcastic.

It's a trait of my species. Please. I'm so bored. Pretty please, with cherries on top?

Very well. Do you by any chance know who Charles Willson Peale is?

Never heard of the guy.

It all starts with him.

The Mammoth Steppe was a vast prairie that stretched halfway around the world. If you began walking at one end as a calf, you would be an adult by the time you arrived at the other. Bunch grass bloomed as far as the eye could see. Which was just as well, given how many animals relied upon it for sustenance. In addition to there being almost a million of us, we shared the plains with thirty million *Bison*, *Equus*, *Camelus*, *Glyptodon*, *Megalonyx*, *Ursa*, *Canis dirus*, and an endless swathe of *Smilodon*, *Panthera* and *Acinonyx*, all of whom were, quite frankly, a pain in the rectum.

The grasslands were punctuated with explosions of colourful flowers: irises and buttercups. They tasted awful. It was perpetually cold and sunny. Perfect weather for ensuring the water remained locked in the glaciers. It hardly ever rained or snowed on the steppe. As far as I was concerned, it was paradise. So, when I died – the reasons for which are complex and much too dramatic to delve into just yet – I lay down on the hard earth and accepted its embrace. I was tired of fighting and welcomed oblivion. My life came to a dignified end.

Little did I know back in 11,347 BC, as the hominids call it, I was in Orange County, New York. The spot I chose as my presumed final resting place became a farm just outside the town of Montgomery. A tiny burgh, by all accounts. Originally settled by German Palatines as Hanover in 1710, the place was apparently renamed after a general who fought in the American Revolutionary War.

I found all this out when Peale dug me up. It was most confusing. I did not recognise any of the placenames and I did not know what a Palatine was. Or a German, for that matter.

There's a pterodactyl next room over. She's from Germany.

This works better if you don't interrupt, *T. bataar*. Once a mammoth builds up a head of steam—

All right, I get it. Keep your furry hat on.

Where was I? Yes, Montgomery. Charles Peale. It is perhaps easier to picture the location of my disinterment by examining the painting Peale created five years later. Since I was somewhat discombobulated at the time, his canvas is a useful point of reference. *Exhumation of the Mastodon* now resides in the Maryland Historical Society's collection, but since we are unlikely to be visiting Baltimore anytime soon, I shall endeavour to describe the scene.

Don't get fancy.

Pardon me?

I'm saying, keep it simple, *Mammut*. You're not delivering a lecture at Harvard.

Do you want to hear about this, or not?

Sure, as long as it's in terms I understand. I only learnt English in Florida last year. Cut me a break, furball.

My apologies, *T. bataar*. I forget you were resurrected a mere sixteen years ago.

I'm just a teenager, really, when you think about it. *Teenage rex.* An immigrant too. This is not my first language, bro.

I'll carry on, shall I?

Yes please. So, there's a painting of you hanging in a Baltimore museum? That's pretty neat.

Let's just say I'm not the centrepiece of Peale's work.

In the painting you can see parts of me, but mostly it's men digging up my bones. At the centre of the painting lies a pit, partially filled with water. A large wigwam frame towers over the hole. Attached to its apex are a series of buckets, running on a pulley system. A waterwheel situated between two windblown trees powers this contraption. A number of hominids stand at the crest of the excavation, observing the men knee deep in the water below. These workers are conveying bones up to their companions – my bones, no less – the discovery of which appears to be a source of amazement. In the background are several tents, and a lightning strike flares in the distance. A bit dramatic, but that was Peale. This biped had a flair for showmanship. He and his family also feature, standing in the foreground, bearing an unfurled sketch of what I am supposed to look like once reassembled. Several of his children are present, though only one of his wives. Given the canvas was painted around 1805, I think it is Hannah More, his third. Thankfully she bore him no offspring. She had her hands full raising the sixteen he had already sired from two previous marriages.

The image is a confection, of course, as is most human art. Although I may not have had my wits about me after finding myself wrenched back from nothingness, I was acutely aware of my surroundings. Details tend to stick in the mind when your eyes are opened for the first time in thirteen millennia.

The scene was quite different to the one portrayed. It was raining, for a start. There was no lightning to imbue Frankenstein's monster with life. Just steady, miserable drizzle. The pit was a cauldron of mud and slime. The waterwheel had broken down and a large hominid was beating at it with a hammer while swearing profusely. Buckets of water were being passed down by hand, although those standing in three feet of fetid, freezing sludge and urine sorely questioned the need for them.

As for Peale, he was there all right, but only when the weather was not inclement. And his brood never accompanied him. Masten, the farmer who uncovered my femur in the first place, wouldn't permit children on the site. He was a tetchy fellow. All he cared about was how much he would be paid for my remains. The newly installed president desperately wanted the skull and tusks of a mammoth so he could prove to the French how great America was. In particular, his late nemesis, Georges-Louis Leclerc, le Comte de Buffon.

Buffon was a naturalist, and in volume five of his seminal book on natural history, imaginatively titled *Histoire Naturelle*, he had taken a swipe at the burgeoning new nation calling itself the United States of America. His Theory of American Degeneracy claimed that animals in America were weaker, smaller and fewer in number than in the rest of the world. 'There is no comparison between the size of the elephant, the rhinoceros, the hippopotamus, the camelopard' – that's a giraffe to you, *T. bataar* – 'the camel, the lion, the tiger, &c. and the tapir, the cabiai, the ant-eater, the lama, the puma, the jaguar, &c. which are the largest quadrupeds of the New World,' he proclaimed. This upset a lot of sensitive new Americans, none more so than founding father Thomas Jefferson.

When Jefferson sailed to Paris in 1784 to represent the new United States, he packed an uncommonly large panther skin with the idea of shaking it under Buffon's nose. Later, he produced a moose. The French were unimpressed. Desperate for America to appear bigger and better than everyone else – and to promote American democracy as the superior form of government – Jefferson hired several groups of hardy pioneers to secure him a mammoth.

Jefferson had heard rumours of large bones found by explorers in various wilderness locations. He convinced himself that they belonged to a mastodon larger than anything that had ever existed in Europe. Indeed, he decided to promote the idea that such a beast still existed in the wilderness. A preposterous notion. My kind, like yours, was long extinct.

In any event, he was willing to pay through the snout for specimens, which is why Mr Masten was so hot under the collar about Mr Peale digging an enormous pit in the middle of his field. This was not the sole excavation underway. The race was on to be the first to provide the president with his coveted monster head. Money was at stake. Favour was there to be curried. Careers were going to be made.

Why was Thomas Jefferson so obsessed with securing my head? You have only been back for sixteen years, my predatory friend. George Bush Senior held the office of president when you were unearthed, as his son does today. You have mostly lived through the Clinton administration. I, on the other hand, have been back on Terra Firma for forty-one of the forty-three commanders in chief. Let me tell you, and I say this as an original American, nothing compares to this nation's willingness to promote patently false notions about itself in order to create a myth of American potency. Politics in this country has at its core an overcompensation for feelings of inadequacy. That is why men self-aggrandise so, and why successive paternalistic leaders have attempted to overcome their inferiority complexes by appropriating symbols of strength from the natural world. Why else are we for sale in this draughty warehouse? Who do you imagine will buy us? You said it yourself, *T. bataar*. We represent power, for that is what we were: Behemoths. Colossi. Titans.

Incidentally, did you know that many adherents to Jefferson's doctrine engaged in similar practices? Republican presidents in particular have been notorious for collecting trophies. It is not giving anything away to reveal Jefferson did wind up with a mammoth skull at the White House, although it was not mine. He also kept two bears as pets. Calvin Coolidge possessed a veritable menagerie, including a hippopotamus, a black bear, and two lions named Tax Reduction and Budget Bureau. John Quincy Adams owned an alligator that lived in a White House bathroom. He found it amusing to surprise guests by sending them in there to defecate. In many cases, they were unable to remove their garments before doing so.

Theodore Roosevelt went much further. During his reign, a lion, a hyena, a coyote, five bears and a zebra lived on the White House grounds. He also shot a reputed eleven thousand, three hundred and ninety-seven creatures. Among them were again lions, but also leopards, cheetah, hyena, elephants and endangered rhinoceroses. These were mounted in a trophy room at the White House and are likely there to this day.

What great men they were! Enslaving and slaughtering our sisters and brothers, perhaps our descendants. What a boon man is to the world, helpfully clearing away its original inhabitants to make room for their grubby dwellings and mewling spawn.

You really have to hand it to them – they've taken a pristine wilderness that spanned the globe and brought it to heel with their concrete and firearms and technology. For this, they must be congratulated. Without their intervention, the world would be little more than a ramshackle, overgrown Arcadia.

I wish I had killed more of them.

Listen, *Mammut*, buddy, it could be worse.

You think so? We are the disembodied spirits of prehistoric beasts, *T. bataar*, condemned to live in the infernal world of bipeds for as long as our body parts remain above ground, instead of crumbling to dust in the earth as they were meant to. We are currently on display in a seedy warehouse, being poked and prodded by all and sundry. Then, once we are sold to the highest bidder, we'll spend our days as museum exhibits, with grotty human children wiping their hands on our bones. How could our humiliation be any deeper?

At least we're not million-year-old fossilised penguins, like the one in with all the smaller exhibits. Have you seen the state of that guy? He's not in good health. Physically or mentally. I've heard they're moving him into the main room with us later. He's not generating much interest out there next to the mummy's hand.

That is obviously stolen from a collection in Egypt. I hope it's cursed.

Apparently she's talking too. Demanding she be reunited with the rest of her body. She and the penguin are driving each other up the wall.

It's the indignity of it all that gets me, *T. bataar*.

Well, on the bright side, the humans won't be around much longer.

What makes you say that?

Asteroids, bro. You just can't plan for them. One minute you're lord of all you survey and the next – BOOM! Space rock impact. Cataclysmic environmental damage. Tidal waves, volcanoes erupting, dust blocking out the sun – the whole shebang. These puny cockroaches don't stand a chance.

How do you know there's one on the way?

It stands to reason, *Mammut*. I mean, it's been a while. Each day that passes where an asteroid doesn't destroy Earth increases the odds of it happening tomorrow, yeah?

I'm not sure that's empirically correct.

I'm telling you, bro. Watch the skies.

Where did you learn to speak English again, *T. bataar*?

I lived in a warehouse in Orlando for nine months. I was in a packing crate, mostly, but I picked it up from the guys who worked there. I've got a pretty good ear. I speak Russian and Spanish too, and a couple of Mongolian dialects: Khalkha and Chakhar. Not much call for those over here.

A little niche, perhaps.

How about you, *Mammut*?

English, French, Spanish, Italian and German, obviously, but also Dutch, Swedish, Norwegian, Afrikaans and a little Gaelic.

That's quite a lot.

One must occupy one's time somehow, *T. bataar*.

Do you speak the old tongue? I mean, the *old* one?

It had probably changed a little by my time, but yes.

That penguin jabbers on in it sometimes. Weird hearing it again. Poor little guy. I think he's lost the plot. I feel bad for him.

I heard one of the bipeds mention there is a *Canis dirus* skull in here somewhere too.

A dire wolf, huh? They were around the same time as you, eh? Maybe you know her, *Mammut*.

It seems unlikely, though I may have enjoyed a familiarity with one of her scions. We shared a compact with her kind for a while.

You made a deal with the wolves? That sounds risky, bro.

They proved honourable. In any event, we had no choice. We were forced to band together against a common enemy.

Oh, I know this one. Man, right?

Yes, my friend. But also, a much greater foe. Time. We ran out of time.

When the Neanderthal arrived on the steppe, they lived alongside us in relative harmony. They were truly stupid. They had at their feet all the materials required for the construction of shelters, and yet it never occurred to them to erect a wikiup. Instead, they fought with bears and lions for prime cave real estate. They hunted *Mammut* too, in their own pathetic way. Their spears were laughable sharpened sticks that bounced off our hides. Their sense of self-preservation was not very evolved. They would rut out in the open, exposing themselves to attack. My grandfather told me he saw a couple torn apart by a pack of *Smilodon* who snuck up on the humans while they were copulating in a woodland glade. Talk about *coitus interruptus*.

We figured if these were the best hairless bipeds nature could throw at us, we would be lords of the steppe for the next million years. Then Clovis turned up. Their numbers were few at first, but we knew immediately they would be trouble. These bipeds were dressed head to toe in animal skins, carefully sewn together with bone needles. It was my introduction to the oddly intertwined human notions of pride and style. Fur was in that season, as it was to be every season thereafter.

If my stomping on one of the Clovis hunters seems cruel, it is worth stating that our numbers dwindled into the thousands after their arrival and subsequent domination of the landscape. The problem was one of natural selection. Clovis singled out mature bulls such as myself for our tusks. They fashioned them into thrones for their chieftains. My species was being wiped out so their leaders would have somewhere nice to sit.

Without the guidance of older males, the immature young bucks ran amok. They fought among themselves and treated the females poorly. Many cows died from injuries sustained while breaking up bulls that had locked tusks. They were too young to be suitable mates, and their progeny withered in the womb. Calves were stillborn. We were extinguishing our own kind.

Fires on the grasslands meant less forage. Trees grew where before there were none, and enormous forests appeared. That may have been great for the birds, but for megafauna? Not so much. It began to rain all the time. The ice receded. Snow fell on the plains, covering the grass in a layer of insulating white powder. It was getting hotter, and wetter.

I called for a powwow. Word went out to whichever old bulls were left standing in the region. We met with the female elders, representing the great herd.

'Too many Clovis, and it's getting too hot,' I told the assembled proboscideans. 'I say we head north and follow the ice.'

Not everyone was convinced this was a good idea, but many agreed to come with me. Most of the younger females came – they were smart enough to see the writing on the wall. The rest thought they could tough it out, that the Clovis expansion would be checked by nature, that balance would be restored. They honestly believed these new hairless bipeds were smart enough not to hunt their food supply to extinction.

They were wrong.

It was quite a thing to see, one thousand head of mammoth striding forth in unison across the steppe. We attracted considerable attention. It had not occurred to me that other species might feel the same anxiety we did concerning our potential annihilation. *Glyptodon* and *Bison* were never the brightest of vertebrates, and so our passage among their numbers was met with shrugs of indifference. *Megalonyx* were too laconic to be bothered even inquiring where we were going. But the beasts of the plains who were fleeter of foot – the *Equus*, *Canis* and felidae – exhibited a definite curiosity towards our mass movement.

The horses were the first to join our procession. It was a wise move, permitting them to come along. They proved a tasty distraction for predators. The noise of so many hooves attracted every big cat and wolf for two hundred leagues. I had never seen so many sabretooth, lions, jaguars, leopards and dire wolves assembled in one place before. Great packs of them snarled about the edges of the herd, flanking us, unsure if they should charge en masse or fight each other. They seemed to settle on a wary armistice in the face of such abundant game.

You know what they say about cats, though. A few foolhardy felidae – and, in some cases, literal lone wolves – couldn't stand the heady scent of such an ambulatory smörgåsbord and waded recklessly into the breach. It did not go well for them. All attempts at separating calves from the herd were rebuffed by a cohort of bulls who at first were irritated by the attacks, but soon warmed to the task of actively taunting the observing packs of drooling carnivores.

Eventually, they sent a cowed envoy, requesting parley. I halted the herd and strode out to meet the alpha cat. An impressive dire wolf stood alongside him, bemused and clearly prepared for betrayal.

'Can I help you with something?' I said.

'If it's not too much trouble,' the *Smilodon* alpha said and purred, affecting nonchalance even though I could tell he was frightened of the much larger dire wolf. 'Would you mind telling us where you're going?'

'Why would I do that?'

'This constant chase is boring me,' said the big *Canis dirus*, yawning. I presume this was an attempt to intimidate me with his fangs. 'We'll run ahead and wait for you to catch up.'

'You'll be nice and tired by then,' said the sabretooth. 'We'll eat you while you sleep.'

'Very considerate,' I told him.

'Consider it professional courtesy,' the wolf said.

'Best start running,' I told them. 'We'll be along in a month or so, if you're still alive.'

The alpha cat and dog looked at each other in a way that I have never seen two representatives of their respective species do since. I put them out of their misery by briefly summarising my intention and rationale.

Canis dirus turned away and looked up at the emerging moon. Crepuscular hour was ending. It would soon be night. *Smilodon* merely scowled, muttering under his breath.

'We've been thinking along similar lines,' the wolf admitted. 'This balmy weather doesn't agree with our kind. We were concerned there'd be no prey, but...' He flashed me an accommodating grin.

'So, tag along,' I said, surprised at my munificence.

'I think we will.'

'What about your lot?' I asked the sulking *Smilodon*.

'Are the *Bison* going?'

'Do you see any *Bison*? I thought cats had good eyesight.'

'Fucking *Mammut*. Piss off, then, to your mythical ice fields of the north. We'll stay here, where lunch is guaranteed. I'm not scared of those puny bipeds. We've dealt with men before. We'll just kill them.'

Canis dirus took a deliberate step away from *Smilodon* towards me, turning as he did so to stand by my side. It was the closest I had ever been to a dire wolf that wasn't trying to devour me.

'The truce is over,' he told the big cat.

'It's like that, huh?'

'Yep. Run along now, kitty.'

'Fuck you.'

The wolf and I watched him lope back to the array of cats, who shook their heads and laughed when he brought them up to speed. They skulked off to a safe distance to watch the herd. I don't confess to understand how *Canis dirus* communicated the instructions to his pack, but they stood up and trotted towards us, coming to a halt at a respectful distance, so as not to spook the *Equus*. It didn't work.

'Were you really thinking of heading north?' I asked the alpha wolf.

'Nah,' he said. 'I just wanted to piss him off. I hate that guy. Good idea, though.'

'Do me a favour and tell your carnivorous cabal to try to stick to the horses.' I didn't expect the wolves to betray their instincts, but it was worth a shot.

'If I promised, would you trust me?'

'About as far as I could toss you.'

'Well, then. I believe we have an arrangement.'

Despite my scepticism, that proved to be a fortuitous day for both our species. We could not save each other, of course. Every four-legged creature that stood on that wide plain was doomed. But, for a while, we kept each other alive. There was still hope, still possibility. We did not know that soon we would all be dead.

We tried a similar thing with *Allosauruses*, bro. It didn't work out. Too many deathmatches. My tail's bigger than yours, I can run faster than you, look at your puny little hands – that sort of thing.

Next thing you know, a couple of rivals are going at it hammer and tongs, ripping literal shreds off each other while the rest of us stand round chanting and making bets. It was fun while it lasted. I witnessed some great scraps, *Mammut*. But interspecies alliances are tough to maintain. Relationships are a lot of work, *hermano*. In the end, it's better if everyone goes their own way. You stay on your side of the volcano; I stay on mine.

For what it's worth, history proclaimed *Tyrannosaurus* as winners. Your reputation for ferocity is unmatched. You are literally the worst creature that ever existed.

Aw, thanks, bro. We do it for the fans, you know?

You said you were exhumed from the Gobi Desert, *T. bataar*?

Yeah, what a mess. I knew something was up as soon as I saw daylight. Straightaway I was like, whoa. Is it hot in here, or is it just me? Pretty sure this was a paradise of humidity last time I checked. And there was crap everywhere, man. Stuff I'd never seen before. Had to take a crash course in human detritus. Empty vodka bottles, turns out, along with crumpled-up cigarette packets and old cars that had been picked clean for parts. I half-expected Mel Gibson to roll up in his supercharger. Hey, by the way, aren't movies great? I mean, if I still had my actual limbs, I'm sure I'd find better ways to entertain myself, but given the circumstances, thank you, Hollywood! And DVD players – wow! Surely that's the apex of human achievement.

My personal favourites, my fearsome friend, are films that attempt to portray the early hominids with whom I am sadly familiar. *Quest for Fire* is amusing. *The Clan of the Cave Bear* is so bad it's good.

I haven't seen either of those! I'll call Blockbuster to put them on hold. I'm a big fan of *The Valley of Gwangi*, myself. *Allosaurus* versus cowboys – what's not to like?

Ripe for a *T. bataar*–starring remake, methinks.

You said it, brother. Anyway, where was I? The Gobi Desert. What a shithole. Maybe I would feel differently about my resurrection if some well-meaning scientists had dug me up, but no, I had to be dragged back to consciousness by a bunch of stinking, grave-robbing fossil poachers. Just my luck to die in sediment rich with uranium too. That's why my bones were so well preserved, *Mammut*.

They're also very white, if you don't mind my saying.

Not at all, bro. It's the radioactivity. Keeps me looking freshly deceased. Lucky, really. It's how the eggheads will be able to work out where I came from, once this sham of a sale is over.

You believe the authorities will notice you are not *Tyrannosaurus rex*?

Mongolia doesn't allow the export of dinosaur bones. I'm an illegal immigrant, buddy. As soon as Homeland Security finds out, I'm on the next cargo plane back to Central Asia.

How did these poachers smuggle you out of Mongolia in the first place, *T. bataar*?

I was a tad confused at the time, bud, given it was my first day above ground in almost seventy million years, so I couldn't swear to this in court, but I think they packed me in with a shipment of coal. Not to disparage the folks back home, but, outside of Ulaanbaatar, Mongolia is dirt poor. Someone was likely slipped a few extra tögrög to look the other way, and that's all it would have taken. What's this, a huge, irradiated dinosaur skull from the desert? Oh no, my mistake, just a bunch of coal. Nice doing business with you.

It had not occurred to me before that you bear the name of your capital city.

Ulaanbaatar means 'Red Hero', so that makes me 'Tyrant Lizard Hero', yeah.

Whereas your American cousin is 'Tyrant Lizard King'.

Hero trumps King.

Forgive my impudence, but is *T. bataar* not slightly smaller than *T. rex*?

Buddy, you wouldn't say that if I were alive. Not to my snout.

Fortunately for me, we have been reduced to skeletal remains. Shadows of our former selves.

There's really very little difference. It's a bit like saying Harvey Keitel is smaller than Robert De Niro. As in, you probably wouldn't. Not if you valued your hide.

So, you haven't seen much of the United States of America – as they so quaintly call it – outside of Florida?

Man, I'm so pumped to be here in New York! I wish I had my legs again. You and me, bro, we'd strut down Fifth Avenue and strike terror into their greedy little hearts. Maybe head over to Central Park for a snack and a quick dip in the pond. See the sights. Live it up!

We can but dream, *T. bataar*. May I ask you a personal question? It's species related, so I hope you don't find it offensive.

Fire away, tusky.

What purpose do your tiny hands serve?

What tiny hands? My hands are huge.

No, they're not. They are comically small.

They're bigger than human hands.

That may be so, but in proportion to the rest of you, they seem unusually feeble.

Says you, *Mammut*.

Says everyone, actually. I have also heard that the size of the hand is directly related to the size of the phallus in certain creatures.

Whoa, buddy, hold your *Equos*. I can assure you I have no problem on that front. No problem at all. I guarantee it.

So, what are they used for, *T. bataar*?

Talking. What else?

Doesn't one usually employ one's mouth for that?

We use them to gesture and explain things. Point stuff out. Like, when you're snout deep in the entrails of an *Ankylosaurus* and someone asks which way to the lake. Over there, buddy. What do *Mammut* use their hands for?

We don't have any.

Well, there you go. Yet again, *T. bataar* wins.

Fortunately, I do not require limbs of any sort to converse, though I will confess to missing my trunk, which frequently proved useful in pressing home a salient point. Now, where was I? Ah yes, above ground and en route to the Athens of America. Philadelphia's decade as the capital city of the United States came to a close just before I decamped there from the

Masten farm, conveyed into town on the back of a buggy in a series of wooden crates. The federal government, which had enjoyed the fruits of local denizen Benjamin Franklin's inventive labours, moved their operations to the District of Columbia in 1800 once the construction of the White House and Capitol Building were complete.

Were Philadelphians glad to see the back of the venal political class? The point is debatable, but for sure one of the most common refrains that sang out to my newly resurrected senses was that locals were relieved to have their city back. The status of capital never sat well with the city's inhabitants, who enjoyed a robust and fruitful relationship with the art of progress. Science, letters and intellectual pursuits were the mainstays of Philadelphian life, championed by men such as Benjamin Franklin and my new benefactor, Charles Peale.

Franklin, incidentally, while famed for inventing the lightning rod, also provided the hominids with bifocal glasses and the urinary catheter. While such items would be useless to me even if I held corporeal form, it is thanks to another of his endeavours that I owe my education in bipedal ways.

Poor Richard's Almanack was an annual magazine written entirely by Benjamin Franklin and published every year between 1732 and 1758. The final edition was issued almost five decades prior to my disinterment, but these pamphlets were widely collected in Philadelphia. Peale's son Rembrandt was an aficionado of Franklin's esoteric ramblings and would read aloud from his collection of almanacks for the edification of lesser-educated employees in the workshop of his father's natural history museum. Which is where I also happened to be housed, while they worked out which bone fitted into which socket. Some assembly was required.

Richard Saunders, or 'Poor Richard' as he was commonly known, made annual pronouncements on the weather, astrology and prominent events in the upcoming calendar. He also spouted witticisms and philosophical aphorisms concerning the nature of man and the tedium of hominid life. The most popular section of the almanack was arguably that in which Poor Richard predicted the deaths of rival astrologers. In addition, he wrote serialised news stories, the narratives of which endured for years.

Saunders was of course Franklin, and in creating this fictional persona the man made himself a small fortune. Or at least enough to further finance his obtuse experiments. He acknowledged the public's contribution to his new-found wealth in the introduction to the 1734 edition of the almanack, wherein he attributed his wife's acquisition of a new cooking pot to their generous patronage.

Suffice it to say, my knowledge of the English language was skewed towards the arcane as a result of listening to Franklin's *bon mots*. While many passed into common parlance, others remained abstruse. Some of my favourites, which you may recognise, even if their origin has remained obscure to you until now, include: 'Don't throw stones at your neighbours, if your own windows are glass'; 'He that speaks much is much mistaken'; and 'Fish and visitors stink in three days.'

To an extent, *Poor Richard's Almanack* proved such a

formative influence on my second life that it inspired me to record this very account.

I know you hate interruptions, *Mammut*, but I have to stop you there. None of this is being recorded, to my knowledge. Unless it is, and I missed the email. T.bataar_xtreme@hotmail.com, in case you were wondering.

I merely meant as in *record* for posterity. It is an oral account, not a written one. I am what the Irish refer to as a *seanchaí*.

A shanniky? What a funny tongue they have.

The *seanchaithe* were oft-itinerant storytellers who preserved history and lore through an oral tradition. Just as *Mammut* have always done, the *seanchaithe* passed their stories from one generation to the next. These tales do not need to be written down in order to be remembered.

It couldn't hurt, though.

Nonsense. *Mammut*, like the Irish, do not forget. Even after I finish telling you this story, I could easily recite it again from memory. Should one of the deluded bipeds suddenly acquire the ability to hear me and choose to document the account, well, more fool them. Franklin may have earned a tidy sum from the publication of his almanack, but no-one gets into the writing game for money these days. No-one in their right mind, at any rate.

I don't know, bro. All this talk is kinda inspiring me to pen a memoir. The moving story of a lonely tyrannosaur who died so cruelly in molten lava. A tale of love, loss and redemption. An uplifting tribute to the struggle—

You're going to write this with your tiny hands? That I'd like to see.

Why is it always with the hands? You know, this is a clear-cut case of workplace bullying.

File a complaint with HR. Now, if you don't mind, I'll continue.

At the time of my arrival in 1801, Peale had been running a museum for fifteen years. An accomplished painter, Peale opened his home on Third and Lombard streets to the paying public. Those willing to part with the requisite coin were privy to portraits of Revolutionary War officers and public figures from the era. This became so popular that he moved the museum into the American Philosophical Society building on Fifth and Chestnut streets in 1794.

When I was carried into the workshop, the sounds that echoed around the halls told me that I had become part of a menagerie. Several flesh-and-bone creatures lived among the stuffed birds and fossils. Two *Ursus arctos*, a simian and a majestic *Haliaeetus leucocephalus* were imprisoned therein. That they housed grizzly bears and a bald eagle in confined spaces speaks volumes about the cruelty of the hominid. Like ourselves, such beasts were meant to roam vast areas of wilderness, not live on the second floor of the American Philosophical Society.

Later, as the museum grew, there would be rooms dedicated to quadrupeds, marine life and yours truly, the American mastodon—

Hold on, I thought you were a woolly mammoth.

Your presumption is understandable, if incorrect. *Mammuthus primigenius*, or the woolly mammoth, is my Russian cousin, generally speaking. I am *Mammut americanum*. We are proboscidean. Elephants, if you will. Virtually indistinguishable, apart from the length of our manes.

Oh. Thanks for clearing that up. In my mind, you're now a lot tastier, minus the shag pile. And, hey, tell me this, is Chestnut Street part of West Philadelphia, by any chance? One of the packers in Florida made a big deal of telling everyone he was from there.

It runs through the centre of town and into West Philadelphia.

So, you're born and raised in West Philadelphia. Did you happen to spend a lot of your days in the playground?

I should have seen that one coming. Most amusing, *T. bataar*, although the irony will be unbearable if I am purchased by some wealthy buffoon from Bel Air.

Ooh, that would be hilarious!

In addition to the displays of artefacts stolen from the indigenous hominids of Fiji, Hawaii and their own western plains, the museum would later house such sensationalist curiosities as a five-legged calf and the trigger finger of a convicted murderer. There were also technical demonstrations of newfangled gadgetry, but more on this matter anon.

The point I am belabouring to make is this: Peale's museum of natural history and portraiture was an eccentric place for a *Mammut* to find himself thirteen thousand years after he sank into the mire. In the museum workshop Peale progeny surrounded me. In addition to the aforementioned Rembrandt Peale, whose love for *Poor Richard's Almanack* served me so well, Rubens Peale, Raphaelle Peale, Franklin Peale and Titian Ramsay Peale were frequently in attendance, although the latter two were mere infants.

Before you butt in again, yes, their father took his obsession with art a little far. Their sisters, with whom I was less familiar, were Angelica Kauffman Peale, Sophonisba Angusciola Peale and Elizabeth De Peyster Peale. They had the good sense to marry their way out of the clan at the first opportunity.

The member of the family I came to know best was Moses Williams, the son of emancipated slaves who was born at roughly the same time as Rembrandt Peale. Those two were thick as thieves and charged by the patriarch with my reconstruction.

'How are we going to do this?' Rembrandt asked his friend.

'Why are you asking me?' Moses replied.

'You're the expert at putting things together.'

'Where'd you get that idea?'

'You repaired those stuffed birds the Finsbury Museum sent us, didn't you?'

'Yes, but that wasn't difficult because I know what a bird looks like. Two wings, a beak, tail feathers – you don't have to be a zooarchaeologist to work it out.'

'True,' Rembrandt said. 'This incognitum is a different proposition.'

'Show me those drawings.'

Rembrandt had in his possession a sheaf of sketches that his father had given him as reference. They were rudimentary and based on guesswork. The truth is, at that time, the exact physical form of *Mammut americanum* remained obscure, as no living biped had ever seen one. Moses laid the papers out on the workshop table and the two young hominids studied them. *Incognitum* was, incidentally, one of the labels bandied about for me during that period. *Unknown*.

'Basically, it's a big pachyderm,' Moses said.

'Looks that way.' Rembrandt nodded. 'I guess that should make it easier.'

'In theory. You ever seen an elephant?'

'You know I haven't. Ain't either of us been further than New York.'

'I went to Braintree, once. To deliver your father's painting of John Hancock to his kin.'

'My commiserations. Where was I?'

'Sick. Bout of fever, as I recall.'

'I often used to fake that to get out of doing chores.'

'How'd you fake fever, Rembrandt?'

'I can control my body temperature.'

'The hell you can.'

'Did you see me on the back of the buggy to Braintree? There you go, then.'

Moses shifted the pages around on the bench in an attempt to make sense of them.

'These are all two-dimensional,' he said. 'Don't see why we can't display this beast lying flat like everything else.'

'Dad wants to make a grand statement by being the first museum to have a freestanding mastodon exhibit. Thinks it'll thrill and terrify the plebs in equal measure.'

'Should turn some coin, for sure. Ain't going to be easy, mind. Can't just stack the bones on top of each other and hope nobody knocks into it.'

'We'll have to devise some means of attaching the joints,' Rembrandt said. 'And maybe rig up some pulleys and high-tension ropes to moor the accursed thing in place.'

'I'm supposing he wants us to present the monster in a dramatic pose, as if it's about to crush one of our ancestors underfoot.'

Oh, Moses. If only you knew.

'You suppose correctly,' Rembrandt told him.

'How long we got to do this?'

'About a month, Dad said. Maybe two. He'd like to be open in the fall.'

'Goddamn. Do we even know if we got a complete skeleton?'

Rembrandt shook his head. 'First thing we gotta do is clean everything and catalogue it. Work out what's missing.'

'I could prob'ly fill in any gaps with clay moulds,' Moses said.

'Let's bust open these crates and get to it then.'

It is fair to say I took a shine to the pair straightaway. They shared an easy familiarity born from decades of intimacy. They had received identical educations and were clad in virtually the same clothes. That their pallor was so very different did not seem remarkable. All bipeds looked the same to me then. It was not until later that I discovered hominids cared so deeply about such matters, and that CW Peale once owned Moses's parents. In fact, according to the law, Moses was still the technical property of CW until he turned twenty-seven, despite the fact his parents won their freedom fifteen years prior. Ownership is a strange, uniquely human notion. The bipeds are obsessed with staking their claim over places, people and things. I cannot understand it. No beast of air, land or sea ever asserted the right of possession over another creature, except to devour it. The hominids don't even eat each other anymore.

Within days my remnants were spread out on the floor of the workshop and I was aware of everything that was going on. I presented something of a jigsaw puzzle for the boys, but they were smart enough to move the major pieces into more or less the correct position. Having a mostly intact skull and tusks helped. At least I had my head about me. The drawings proved useful and when CW visited to check on their progress, he evinced delight in their ability to solve the conundrum. I was to be his star exhibit.

In stating that Rembrandt and Moses had identical educations, I am omitting one crucial detail. The boys may have been equals in wit and science, but only Rembrandt and his siblings were trained in the high arts, which is to say painting. At that period in history, no American of African origin was deemed fit to hold a brush and palette. Ironic in the case of young Moses, traded as an infant to CW by a plantation owner in Maryland in lieu of payment for her portrait.

This embarrassing state of affairs played on Rembrandt's mind, especially given the obvious artistic talent of the man he considered a brother. Of the duo, Moses possessed a more practical mien, disposed as he was to the restoration of natural history exhibits. CW was not aware of the way in which Moses applied ochres and oils to the plumage of stuffed birds damaged in transit from England.

It was around the time of my arrival that CW acquired another of the gadgets that so fascinated the man: the physiognotrace. This device replicated the outline of a subject's face and created hollow-cut paper silhouettes. CW could make neither head nor tail of the overly complex contraption. The machine was sent to the workshop, whereupon it became the pet project of Moses Williams.

'Have you worked that thing out yet?' Rembrandt asked.

My skull had been refurbished by this stage and was propped upright on the floor. Behind me lay my spinal column, with my ribs and legs fanning out on each side. There were a few gaps still to be filled in, but I was seventy-five per cent complete. It appeared as if I had been squashed by some great force, my belly split open. In other words, I looked ridiculous.

'It's functioning,' Moses said. 'But the silhouettes it produces are inexact. They all look much the same.'

'Not enough detail to distinguish the subjects.'

'Exactly.' Moses chewed his upper lip and scoured the bench for a pair of small scissors. 'Still. No reason why someone couldn't refine them by hand.' He retrieved a rejected silhouette from a pile of papers. 'Turn sideways a minute,' he said to Rembrandt.

'Is that one of me?'

'If you can call this lumpen mass you, then yes. Let me make a few adjustments.'

Glancing between Rembrandt and the piece of paper, Moses trimmed the edges of the silhouette until it more closely resembled his colleague.

'There. How's that?' He handed the finished silhouette to Rembrandt, who held it up against his profile.

'Hey, that's not bad. Pretty good likeness.'

'Don't tear it. You're supposed to mount it on a background of black paper or silk.'

'Sign it for me, Moses.'

Moses took the pencil stub from behind his ear and scribbled his signature on the piece of cut paper.

'I'm sure it will be worth a fortune someday,' he said.

Although I was not there to see it – the reasons for which will become apparent much later, if you can remain awake – I heard that within a year Moses had gained such a reputation for dexterity and accuracy with his hand-altered physiognotrace silhouettes that CW manumitted him in advance of his twenty-seventh birthday and charged him with operating the machine in the foyer of the museum. It cost eight cents to have one's silhouette cut by Moses Williams, a fee that, upon CW's insistence, Moses solely retained.

To his patron's chagrin, the device became the main attraction of the museum. Patrons flocked not to see Peale's stuffy portraits of George Washington, but to have their profiles cut by the affable young man at the entrance. In the first year of operation, Moses produced eight thousand silhouettes. Not long after, he purchased a two-storey house and married.

But we are getting ahead of ourselves. The Moses I knew applied his skills at converting two dimensions into three, and vice versa, to the erection of my mighty frame. The time of my first presentation to the public was fast approaching and there was much to do. It is not every day that a behemoth such as I returns to walk the earth. I was about to cause a sensation.

Can I jump in? Honestly, bro. Take a breather. I knew this was going to be a long story, but I didn't realise it would be so *boring*.

I'm sorry you feel that way, *T. bataar*.

I don't mean to be rude, but a couple more jokes wouldn't go amiss.

My sense of humour is a little drier than yours, I fear.

I want to hear about your adventures, *Mammut*. Not all this stale historical jibber jabber. Tell me more about the great herd and its journey north. Don't leave me hanging, buddy. What about the dire wolves and all the fighting? That's the real juice.

You certainly have a voracious appetite for carnage, *T. bataar*. Very well. I shall return briefly to the story of our pilgrimage to the icy wastes.

Goody. Hey, before you start, did you hear what's happening tonight?

Don't tell me you've organised a jailbreak.

I wish. No, apparently the bipeds are moving all the exhibits for sale in with us later. It's going to be crowded. There won't be room to swing a sabretooth in here, *Mammut*.

Why are they doing that?

The auction takes place next door tomorrow. They need to clear the room so they can put in chairs and a stage.

How did you find this out?

One of the bipeds in charge came through before and was talking about it on his walkie-talkie thing.

I didn't notice.

You were busy monologuing, *Mammut.*

I thought you were listening to me, not eavesdropping on the chitchat of hominids.

I caught most of it, bro. Something about a workshop and a dude called Moses.

Shall I start again from the beginning?

Nah, I got the gist.

I should press ahead, if we are to have company tonight. I don't wish to shout over the cacophony.

Three hundred and forty-five items up for grabs, you know. Mostly animals like ourselves, but also a sixty-two-ounce gold nugget from Australia and a meteorite from Mars, apparently. I'm looking forward to meeting those guys.

They are capable of speech?

A regular comedy duo, I hear.

How is it possible for inert minerals to be witty conversationalists, *T. bataar*?

If you're asking me to explain the science, I'm a little hazy on the specifics. Something to do with collectives of microorganisms embedded deep within the rocks.

Vast cosmic forces at play.

Err ... yep. That must be it.

So, the felidae elected to remain in warmer climes, while *Canis dirus* chose to accompany us on the journey north.

Right. Take it from there, buddy.

Although such a trek might seem arduous, in reality it was rather enjoyable. We were a migratory species that spent its life meandering between woodland and open plain, never worrying about where we were or if there might be enough forage. Nature was not something we ever questioned, which made it all the stranger when she seemed to be turning against us.

The wolves proved to be good company. The horses were terrified of them, of course, but food was plentiful along the way and so *Canis dirus* did not devour as many *Equus* as anticipated. Horses are fleet of foot, and wolves, while dogged in their pursuit of prey, cannot match them for speed. They also become easily bored.

The alpha wolf and I became friends, after a fashion. In the evenings, when the herd halted to rest, he would appear at the edge of our encampment and request an audience. Initially, he was escorted to my location by several wary bulls, but after a few weeks I discharged them from such duties. He was not about to jeopardise our arrangement by snatching a young *Mammut* in his jaws and heading for the hills. Good luck doing that anyway. He may have been big, but we were bigger. Even a calf could impale him with its tusks.

He exhibited no fear when he sat among us, despite being utterly surrounded. I soon came to anticipate our talks, for he was a laconic orator who told stories in a matter-of-fact way that pleased me. In essence, he and his pack acted as our vanguard, running ahead to uncover trails we might follow and alerting us to obstacles that would prove impassable for a herd of such magnitude. Without such reconnaissance, we may well have ambled to our doom.

'A fine evening, my lupine friend,' I said to him.

'The moon is high and the pack roams abroad,' he replied. 'There is no greater time to be alive.'

'What news from the trail?'

'Unforeseen changes in the landscape.'

'Of what nature?'

'The glaciers are leaking. We found a river a few leagues ahead. It was not there last time I came this way.'

'Is it passable?'

'Perhaps. For the moment, it is not deep. The calves may struggle, but it should present little obstacle for the *Equus* and adult *Mammut*.'

'What about *Canis dirus*?'

The dire wolf lay down, placing his head on his front paws. He yawned.

'We could swim, but I'd rather not. We may have to separate for a while, until we find a way across downstream.'

'How big is this river?'

'Pretty big. And there's still a lot of ice held in those glaciers. If that melts, we'll need to make friends with the cetaceans.'

I considered this information for a while before speaking.

'Will there be any of the frozen tundra left when we get there? Surely it cannot all melt away.'

'I'm just saying, swimming lessons might be in order. Just as well the cats didn't come. They would have hated it.'

We talked some more about the changes we had witnessed in our lives before *Canis dirus* roused himself and returned to his waiting pack. They paused on a nearby ridge and, although it was a distance away, I could make out the leader's silhouette against the backdrop of the rising moon. He turned towards the herd, threw his head back and howled. The others joined him in a mournful chorus. Normally, this sound would have struck fear into the hearts of warm-blooded mammals within earshot, but on this night their cries were plaintive, their ululations tinged with regret. Our world was changing and there was nothing we could do about it. Their song of sorrow complete, the pack loped away over the crest of the hill and was swallowed by the darkness.

The next morning, I gathered the elder *Mammut* to explain the situation. The cows were concerned for the safety of the young. I reassured them we would find a solution to assist the calves in the river crossing.

'Yes, but what?' one of the females asked. I recognised her as a mate of mine from several years hence. The curved tip of her left tusk was missing. We had not spoken much since. Bull *Mammut* either kept to themselves upon reaching maturity, or lived in small groups with other males, assuming they got along. That was never really my scene.

'Perhaps we carry them on our backs,' I suggested.

44

There were murmurs of disbelief. It was not our way, though I had witnessed many other creatures employ the technique.

'The calves will love that,' she said.

'Are you being sarcastic?' I asked.

'No, they genuinely will,' she said. 'I know you bulls don't have anything to do with raising your offspring, so perhaps in the process a few of you could be acquainted with your progeny.'

'I am amenable to the notion,' I said, which caused further harrumphing from the old-fashioned bulls among us.

'Good,' she said. 'In that case, come with me and I will introduce you to your son.'

This caught me somewhat unawares.

'Oh,' I said. 'I have a son?'

'You have many, no doubt,' she said. 'This is the one you sired with me.'

'We have a calf,' I stated, rather obviously. Of course, I knew it must be so. I had done my fair share of rutting over the years, though I was never as obsessed as some rampant bulls. She did her best *Mammut* approximation of an eye roll.

'Yup. Thanks for checking in. Typical bull.'

'I always thought of myself as atypical, actually.'

'Well, explain that to your boy. He's been telling all his friends about his father, the great herd commander who's leading us to the promised land.'

'That is unfortunate. We may be marching to our deaths.'

'Yeah, don't tell him that part. The poor kid admires you.'

The brief council meeting was adjourned, accompanied by the

usual mumbling and grumbling. The female indicated I should follow her. Oddly for me, I was apprehensive, and felt compelled to engage in small talk.

'What, uh, happened to your tusk?' I asked.

'Got caught in the midst of a fight between two young bulls,' she said.

'Over you?'

'Yes, over me. Is that so surprising?'

'Not at all. I recall fighting over you myself not so long ago.'

'The old ones knew not to half-kill each other and the cow in the process. There's a serious lack of father figures around here these days.'

I agreed with this, of course. The entire point of me organising the trek north was the preservation of our species. It heartened me to know other *Mammut* were similarly motivated, and that a new generation was accompanying us. Including, in an unexpected and pleasing development, my own son.

The cow pointed him out. The boy was cavorting next to the waterhole with a number of his contemporaries. He was a strong little bull, his tusks already grown to a prodigious size for one so young. A flush of pride surged through my bones.

'A virile specimen of youth, as might be expected.'

The cow merely shook her head in what appeared to be mild disgust.

'Would you like to meet him?'

'I don't think we need go that far,' I said. 'Perhaps later, when I am not so busy.'

Fording the new river would be a time-consuming and dangerous undertaking, or so I thought. As it turned out, the tributary was nowhere near as deep and foreboding as *Canis dirus* had made it out to be. The calves were able to cross under their own prerogative, without the need of assistance from bulls like me. My boy was disappointed that he did not get to ride aloft my shoulders, but I was not about to make a spectacle of myself in front of the entire herd. Also, I did not wish to single him out for special treatment. When he came to ask if I could lift him up onto my back using my trunk, I chided him.

'Don't be a fool,' I told him. 'If you had been a newborn, perhaps, but at your age? Ridiculous. How old are you anyway?'

'Five,' he said, dragging his trunk dejectedly.

'Old enough to know better,' I said, upon which he trotted back to his mother, chastened.

The wolves, who were simply averse to swimming, returned the day after we crossed the admittedly freezing river. They seemed rather pleased we had not been swept away in the deluge.

'We crossed without incident,' I told the alpha. 'It was rather easy, in fact.'

'Even easier on the ice bridge downstream,' *Canis dirus* said, shaking snow from his fur. 'Hardly got my paws wet.'

'I am pleased to hear it,' I told him. 'I would not wish for you to be uncomfortable.'

He ignored my jibe. Wolves have a tendency to take things literally, so he may have thought I was being sincere.

'Another slight problem has arisen,' he told me. 'Clovis.'

'This far north?' I said. 'Surely not.'

'A whole village of them. We spotted their smoke and went to investigate. Quite the sprawling encampment they have going on. Fences and everything. Many huts. And I hate to tell you this, but there was a beautiful long set of tusks mounted at the entrance. They didn't look old, either.'

I ground my molars at the thought of these savages banding together to murder some old friend of mine who had walked the steppe longer than any of them had been alive.

'Were you able to estimate their numbers?' I asked the alpha wolf.

He looked at me askance. 'What do you take me for?' He told me how many Clovis there were, in the ancient tongue. The hominid system of numbers is woefully inadequate for accurate counting.

'That is a lot,' I said. 'I had no idea there were so many of them out here.'

'We've seen camps all over,' *Canis dirus* told me. 'Some bigger than this. I fear we are entering the age of man.'

The thought had occurred to me. 'Soon there will be no room left for the likes of us.'

The big wolf curled his top lip to show me his fangs. 'Well, I don't know about you, but I intend to go down fighting.'

'Can we skirt their camp?'

'Even if we could, it's too late now. They probably have scouts up on that hill, watching us as we speak. They'll report back tonight and there will be hunting parties coming after the calves at first light.'

'Not just the calves,' I said.

'No, but they will start with them. The pack will do what we can to protect the young ones, but we need to come up with a plan or we'll all be roasting on spits by evening.'

All I could think about was killing them. These Clovis were wily. They would keep their distance and pick us off with their long spears or drive us into a canyon and hem us in, to be consumed at their leisure. A pack of *Canis dirus* would present a fearsome opponent, but if the alpha were slain, I could not depend on the beta to stand his ground. He did not approve of the agreement we had made and would likely turn tail and run. I could not blame him. Preservation of his own species. Why should they sacrifice themselves to save a few dozen baby *Mammut*, whom they would gladly have devoured in different circumstances?

However, we did possess one huge advantage over Clovis. We were considerably larger than the bipeds, and there were a lot of us in the herd. Together that represented a considerable mass, which, once it reached a certain velocity, would not be easy to halt.

'We'll stampede right through their village and destroy everything,' I told the alpha wolf. 'How's that for a plan?'

'I like your style, *Mammut*. We'll run with you.'

'Is it far from here?' I asked him.

'Not far,' he said, looking up at the sun overhead. 'If we mobilise the herd now, we could reach their camp tonight.'

I scraped my foot in the dirt and shook my head as if ready to charge. He realised then what I was thinking.

'Hominids fear the dark,' he said, nodding sagely. 'Yes, yes, if we attack while they sleep, they will scatter in the confusion. The herd and horses can break through, while the pack rips the gizzards from their warriors. This is a good plan, *Mammut*.'

'Is the path clear?' I asked. 'Does any impediment lie in our way?'

'There's a lot of water on the ground,' the wolf told me. 'Tributaries and streams formed by the melting glacier, but nothing of consequence.'

'Then we begin the march,' I said. 'Any Clovis that get in our way will be trampled underfoot.'

The alpha yawned. 'Sorry,' he said. 'I don't mean to dilute the drama of the moment. We've been on the hunt all day. The pack will rest here and catch up with you at the village.'

'Don't be late,' I told him.

'I wouldn't miss it for the world,' he said.

We left *Canis dirus* to sleep and began our exodus to the north. As the herd marched onwards, I moved among the *Mammut*, informing them of our strategy. There were no complaints. Everyone had lost kin to the Clovis hunters. When it came to it, not one *Mammut* would hesitate to crush the bipeds underfoot. Their primitive huts, their campfires, even their children would be ground into the tundra. We would grant them no mercy. None could be afforded in the fight for survival.

As I passed through the ranks, I came across my son and his mother. He peered up at me cautiously from beneath her belly. He seemed so very vulnerable. The fate of our calves during such a bold manoeuvre was in question. They could easily stumble and be trampled by our own feet. I decided to assign a platoon of bulls to surround the young ones. With luck, they would remain in the calm eye of the storm, while around them chaos reigned.

'You should come to the front with me,' I told his mother.

'So we can die first? No thanks,' she said.

'It will be safer,' I told her. 'I will protect you both.'

'I want to go,' the boy said, emerging from his mother's shadow. He was a fraction of my size, but he held his nascent tusks up proudly. 'I will fight Clovis.'

'You'll do no such thing,' his mother said, wrapping her trunk around him and trying to pull him close.

The boy squirmed out of her grasp and stepped to my foreleg.

I turned my gaze down towards him.

'I want to stand with you, Father.'

'Truly, you are my son,' I said to him, a lump in my throat. Doubtless some of the couch grass I had been ruminating that morning. Sometimes it is not easy to swallow.

His mother went along with the arrangement, and they took their place at the front of the herd. My thinking was that we would catch Clovis unawares and they would be through the camp before a spear could be thrown. That way, at least my son would survive. I myself did not expect to see another dawn. As commander of the herd, I intended to stand my ground in the midst of the Clovis village, wreaking havoc and drawing as many of the spear points to me as possible. As long as I killed dozens of Clovis, I did not care for my own fate. The herd would endure. *Mammut* would live on. The time for me to join my ancestors was nigh.

Darkness fell as we neared the village. There was still no sign

51

of *Canis dirus*. No matter. We could achieve our goal without them. I halted the herd, so they might rest briefly and gather their thoughts before our assault.

Clovis lived in the lee of the glacier. A sheer wall of ice towered over the herd, casting its cold shadow across the steppe. Water cascaded out of holes in the wall and pooled about our feet. Sections of ice fell away, tumbling down to shatter on the ground below. I had never seen the glacier so fragile.

Despite my intention to wait a little longer to allow *Canis dirus* time to catch up, my hand was forced by a small party of Clovis. They stood atop a crest to the herd's left, leaping up and down and brandishing their spears menacingly. They looked like idiots, but when they began to descend towards us, I decided enough was enough. I lumbered to the front of the herd, raised my trunk in the air and trumpeted for the charge to commence. The hunters fled in alarm at the sound of a thousand trunks joining me in a chorus of anger.

What a joyous noise we made. Thousands of strong feet pounding the tundra as we stampeded into their pathetic village. We were like a river, seeking the path of least resistance as it flowed across the frozen plain. I smashed the gateway of tusks and hurtled onwards. All around me, Clovis ran for their lives, abandoning their huts to flee for the hills. They did not make it. We stamped and tossed and gored our way through their ranks. It was glorious.

The clever ones gathered up their spears and scurried for the high ground to regroup. I saw them massing on the southern slope of their encampment. Boxed in by the glacial cliffs to the north, the herd flowed smoothly through the narrow space. As their huts fell away and I emerged through the far side of the Clovis camp, I slowed and turned to observe what those sneaky devils were up to.

The bulls protecting the young passed through. I knew they were safe. My concern shifted to those *Mammut* at the back of the herd. The old ones, slower than the rest. They would be easy pickings for the Clovis who would attack from the rear. I could not let them fall. Their knowledge was too great.

The herd glided around me like a flock of birds as I re-entered the village. Clovis was on the move. They had recovered from the initial shock and were organising themselves to strike back. A group of warriors waited for their opportunity. I saw from their hand gestures that they intended to divide the rear of the herd and channel a number of *Mammut* to the southeast, where they would be isolated for the slaughter.

Never mind that their families were being trampled. All these men could think of was killing for meat and trophy.

No, I thought. You will not hurt them. If you wish to fight, here I am. You call yourselves men? Prove your worth or die.

I charged into the fray, trumpeting and shaking my great tusks from side to side. The warriors did not expect one of our kind to understand their intention. They thought we were big, dumb beasts. I intended to disavow them of that notion.

I trampled two who stood their ground. Their bones crumbled under my feet. Their chests burst open. I caught another on the sharp tip of my right tusk, piercing his belly. He screamed and spat crimson. With a flick of my neck, I threw him among his companions. That enraged them, and they responded with a barrage of spears.

Several pierced my hide, but I did not stop. They threw more. I was ready this time and batted them away with my tusks. I could see the fear in their eyes now. They knew I was going to kill them all.

A glance over my shoulder. The herd was almost through. Only a few *Mammut* remained, lumbering across the wasteland that had once been a Clovis village. A lone *Equus* reared, kicking its hooves at a Clovis woman. The plan had worked. Victory was close.

A young *Mammut* emerged from the herd, trumpeting as he ran to join me in the struggle against the hunters. A cow appeared at his heels, pleading with him to come back. My son. His mother. I should not have been surprised, but I was. The boy was good to his word. My blood flowed in his veins. He did not want this day to end without doing his part.

Alas, foolish child.

A group of Clovis shadowed them on the slope above. One filthy hominid hefted a long bone knife. He sped down the incline towards my boy, with murder in his eyes.

Ignoring the pain of more spears in my flank, I wheeled about and charged towards my son. He saw me and trumpeted, oblivious to the danger. The Clovis sprang up onto a rock and launched himself into the air, dagger held high in both hands. I could not make it. I could not cover the distance in time. All I could see was the glinting knife, carved from the femur of a *Mammut*.

The biped landed on my son's back. The unexpected impact caused the boy to stumble. His front legs gave way beneath him and he fell, the Clovis clinging to his ears. This bought a few more seconds, but it was still not enough for me to reach him. As the boy squirmed on the ground, the hominid raised his knife to strike.

Then: a flash of white. A guttural snarl. The unmistakable snapping of powerful jaws.

Canis dirus. The alpha, running at full pelt, slammed into the Clovis man, knocking him from my son's prone form. A spray of blood. A gargled scream. A cry of pain.

The alpha wolf stepped back from the spasming body of the biped. The man's throat had been torn out. Gore dripped from the fangs of the wolf. He turned to me, a crazed expression in his eyes. He was panting hard from the exertion of running.

I looked down at the pool of blood forming beneath *Canis dirus* and followed the drips upwards to a wound in his belly, from which the bone knife protruded. He noticed it himself, and angrily gripped the hilt of the dagger between his teeth. He pulled it out, dropped it and howled, blood staining his fur, then turned away and charged towards the group of Clovis with whom I had just been fighting.

The boy's mother scooped him up with her trunk and helped him to his feet. He was dazed, but unhurt.

'Go,' I called to them. 'Join the others.'

My son's eyes were wide as he watched me charge into the fray, scattering Clovis and joining *Canis dirus* in battle. If his mother ushered him away, I never knew. It was the last time I ever saw my son.

The rest of the wolf pack arrived in due course and set about the Clovis hunters. The hominids fought bravely, I'll grant them that, but there was no hope for them. We were set on our path and would not stop until all were dead. Several of the pack fell to Clovis spears but soon we had the numbers to overwhelm them. They had nowhere to run. In truth, I revelled in the killing. I know that is wrong, but those were different times. They were the enemy. We had done them no harm and yet they declared war upon us, the animals of the steppe. What did they expect to happen? That we would lie down meekly for the slaughter? They believed themselves better than us, higher life forms with greater intelligence. They thought dominance was their birthright.

We showed them they were wrong. Clovis are all dead and I'm still here. Somehow, I'm still here.

Despite our injuries, it is possible most of us might have survived, were it not for an unforeseen and ironic circumstance. Several thousand head of *Mammut* stampeding through the Clovis village may have been a monumental event to behold, but it was also a seismic one.

The vibrations caused by the herd travelled through the frozen tundra and into the glacier that loomed over us. The wall of ice was already weakened by heat and water pressure. It was only a matter of time before it crumbled. Our charge merely hastened nature along its course.

As *Canis dirus* and I stood over the last of the dying Clovis, our coats stained with blood, we heard an almighty crack. I looked up at the glacier, then across to my herd. They were standing directly under the ice, catching their breath after the charge. The vast glacier stretched into the distance. No amount of running would save us.

The alpha stood by my side. His breathing was ragged. He had lost a lot of blood. His snout and face were red with Clovis viscera. He began to laugh, low at first, then harder, his entire body shaking. Wolves love irony and majestic deaths.

'*Mammut*,' he said. 'It's been a pleasure running with you.'

I nodded. 'Look at that. What an incredible sight.'

'Once in a lifetime,' he replied, and then the glacier shattered, and the water burst forth. Huge blocks of ice tumbled down, and a wave fell upon us. A freezing sea suddenly released upon the land. Boulders, trees, the remnants of the Clovis village, the great herd of *Mammut*, the pack of *Canis dirus* and all the bodies of the dead were washed away, scattered, obliterated ...

Since you've gone quiet, *Mammut*, I take it you won't mind if I say something?

The memory is painful, *T. bataar*. I require a moment, but you may speak.

If it's any consolation, something similarly catastrophic happened to me.

Were you not consumed by molten lava after a mortal injury?

Well, sort of. I was down and hurt badly, see, but as soon as that hot stuff touched my foot, boy, did I wake up! Buddy, I crawled and hobbled my way out of there. Admittedly, I didn't get far. I'd lost a lot of blood and eventually the old pins gave way but by that time I was clear of the flow. Don't get me wrong, I still popped my clogs but at least I wasn't burnt to death. That would be quite painful, wouldn't it? I died from my injuries and sank into the bog. Not as dramatic as you getting slammed by floodwaters.

My story is not yet complete, *T. bataar*. There is a little more to tell.

Sure, but you've ceded the floor for the moment, so let me get a word in, eh, bud?

If you must.

So pretty soon the raptors picked my flesh clean. Then it rained for a couple of weeks and that washed my bones nicely. Bit by bit, my sorry carcass merged with the earth. I settled into the soil. Wormed my way down beneath the surface, out of harm's way. It was nice and cool down there. Calming, you know? Like doing yoga, minus the back bends. Anyway, as you know, once you're buried, that's it. You're dead. And your soul, or whatever, drifts away to who knows where. The hominids believe you go to Heaven, or Hell, or Purgatory, or Shangri-La, or Zion – I don't know, they have a million names for it. Couldn't tell you if any of them are real. Maybe they simply don't admit dinosaurs and megafauna. You'd think we'd have our own versions but nope. You're just absent. Gone. In the wind.

I mean, as far as I was concerned, *Mammut*, that was it. Never heard no different. What changed my mind was the asteroid. Remember how I told you to watch for those? I cannot stress this point enough. A big one arrived about two million years after I carked it and slammed into Earth – BOOM! That thing came down hard. Must have made one hell of a crater. All the dirt and water and whichever poor schmucks happened to be standing around chewing the cud and minding their own business suddenly found themselves up in the air – WHOOSH! The biggest, swirlingest hurricane the world had ever seen and we're all flying, the living and the dead, except now pretty much everything is dead, obviously. You can't throw a *Brontosaurus* two thousand feet in the air and expect him to land safely on his feet next town over. No, that was it for us. Dead, dead, dead. An extinction-level event, the hominids call it. An ELE. Pretty cool, as long as it ain't happening to you. They'll get theirs eventually. Then who'll be laughing?

No-one.

Right, except us, maybe. Funny thing, though. When I exhaled that last breath two million years prior, I was certain there was no coming back. Yet there I was, my weary bones wrenched from their final resting place, floating around in the atmosphere with every other poor sap. I clearly remember thinking: Huh? That's weird. I thought I was shot of this place.

And then I thought: Ooh. Looks like trouble. The world is literally shifting on its axis. Wow. Wonder how this is going to pan out?

Then I thought: Whee! Woo-hoo! This is *fun*.

No clue what was going on, really. A passing *Stegosaurus* skull wasn't enjoying the ride quite as much.

'Hey, bud,' I called to him. 'What is this? What happened?'

'ASTEROID,' he said. The dude was alarmed, to say the least.

'What's an asteroid?' I asked.

'A big rock fell from the stars,' he told me. 'The world's ending!'

'From the stars? No way.'

'Look at that wave of destruction sweeping across the planet,' he said. 'How can you be so calm?'

'I often wonder that,' I told him. 'Nothing seems to faze me. I guess I'm just a chill guy.'

'Pretty easy being serene when you're top of the food chain. You didn't spend your life looking over your shoulder.'

'Maybe that's it,' I said. 'My biggest concern was always: whom am I going to eat next? Hey, how is it that we can hear each other, anyway?'

'This is hardly the time for a metaphysical debate,' the *Stegosaurus* said. 'Look out below!'

And then – WHAMMO. I hit the ground so fast I broke several teeth. Ploughed into the mud and only had a second to think about it before several tonnes of dirt landed on top of me and everything went black. When I came to, sixty-six million years had elapsed, and some asshole was digging me up out of the Mongolian desert. Bit jarring, really. No idea how my flying *Stegosaurus* buddy fared. I hope it worked out okay for him. He seemed a tad jittery. Trait of the species, I guess. Maybe he's above ground again now too.

Anyhoo, it's no collapsed glacier causing a minor flood, but I thought I'd mention it. So, you were saying there's even more to this story of yours? Really, *Mammut*?

It pales in comparison to your ancient apocalypse, *T. bataar*, but I assure you, the tale is almost at an end. However, the telling of it has disquieted me somewhat, so perhaps I will pick up the thread of my nineteenth-century reconstruction first and return to my demise later. Unless you have some objection.

I did have tickets to see *Hamilton*, but something tells me I'm not going to make it. Do your worst, buddy.

The unfortunate Moses Williams may have been a silhouette artist, a man of learning and unexpectedly gifted in regard to the reconstruction of long-dead megafauna, but as I mentioned earlier, he was also a man of colour. This was 1801, let me remind you, and he had not yet technically shucked off the yoke of slavery. CW Peale still had legal ownership of the young fellow.

Which is why he was so humiliated during the promotion of the mastodon exhibit. Wishing to drum up business for my grand unveiling, CW had Moses pose as a Native American Indian, complete with elaborate headdress, and parade through the streets of Philadelphia riding a white horse. Rembrandt, dressed more modestly in a soldier's uniform, rode alongside playing the bugle to attract attention. Flyers were printed and passed out among the crowds, while Moses proclaimed thusly:

'Ten thousand moons ago, a mighty creature roamed the gloomy forests of our nation. The beast was huge as a frowning precipice, cruel as the bloody panther. With wanton fury it stalked the plains and thunder rolled in its wake. Renowned naturalist and world-famous portraitist Charles Willson Peale has, for the first time in history, recovered the skeleton of this uncanny fiend the incognitum. Be among the first humans to lay eyes upon the mighty MAMMOTH, the largest of terrestrial beings! All who dare are invited to visit Mr Peale's museum, located on the second floor of the American Philosophical Society, on Fifth and Chestnut.'

Although Moses failed to mention it in his oration, the printed flyers included an asterisk at the end of the text. This corresponded to an addendum in extremely small print at the base of the document, which read:

*In addition to the Museum admission fee, entry to the Mammoth Room is charged at the additional rate of 50c per visitor.

Fifty cents was a lot of money back then, but it did not deter the hominids of Philadelphia from turning up in droves. The exhibit was an enormous success. They came from far and wide to gaze upon my bones, a state of affairs that both amused me and provided me with ample opportunity to study the mores, fashions and gossip of the day. I learnt a lot during those months on display, even if my tusks had been mounted upside down. Moses advised CW of this anatomical error, but he disregarded the boy's advice. He thought I looked more fearsome with my tusks inverted, the better to skewer my prey.

As it turned out, ordinary Americans shared Peale's and Jefferson's passion for bigness. I represented American might, and this struck a chord in the new democracy. Within months, everything was mammoth themed. A twenty-pound vegetable grown in New York was proclaimed as a Mammoth Radish. In Washington, a fellow labelled himself a Mammoth Eater after digesting forty-two *Gallus gallus domesticus* eggs in ten minutes.

In the town of Cheshire, Massachusetts, Baptist pastor John Leland was so impressed by Thomas Jefferson's efforts in promoting republicanism and religious freedom that he asked the women of his congregation to produce a Mammoth Cheese as a gift for the president.

Utilising the milk of nine hundred *Bos taurus*, the cheese was constructed in a cider press, in which the typically Jeffersonian maxim 'Rebellion to tyrants is obedience to God' was carved. The Baptists sang hymns over the milk and curds, resulting in the creation of what was, as far as anyone knew, the largest cheese ever created by hominids at that time. It weighed one thousand, two hundred and thirty-five pounds, was four feet wide and fifteen inches thick.

All of which made *le grand fromage* much too large to transport. In order for the cheese to be presented to President Jefferson, it had to be loaded onto a sleigh and dragged from Massachusetts to the Hudson River, whereupon it was taken by sloop to New York and Baltimore. From there, the big cheese was conveyed by wagon to Washington, arriving a few days before the end of the year. Jefferson and his family had it for lunch on New Year's Day, 1802.

Not wishing to accept gifts for fear of appearing corrupt, Jefferson insisted on paying John Leland two hundred dollars for the cheese, a princely sum for the age. His kin were still reported to be eating it the following New Year's Day, although I heard many moons later that it turned sour after that and was discreetly dumped in the Potomac.

Suffice it to say, my unveiling to the unwashed masses

caused a degree of hysteria and consternation. It could not have been timed better for President Jefferson. His fascination with the notion that America had been and could be once again greater than Europe had long been a source of bemusement to his detractors. They thought the man a fool for obsessing over the myth of the American elephant, and yet there I was, in bone if not in flesh. The election had been a close-run thing, with incumbent John Adams narrowly defeated by his deputy. Critics now faded into obscurity as the public embraced Jefferson's dogma of American vigour. Here was the proof! The continent once had its very own titans, the equal to any creature that stalked the woodlands of Europe or prowled the African savannah. And although the precise dating of fossils was still in its infancy, scholars believed my remains to be at least ten thousand years old.

This estimate was more or less correct. If they could hear a word I said, I would gladly have apprised them of the fact my death had occurred precisely thirteen thousand, one hundred and forty-eight years prior to 1801. Sadly, my attempts at conversation fell on deaf ears.

Either way, they were troubling figures. I had come to learn that, rather than rely upon *Poor Richard's Almanack* for their lessons, hominids held in enormous esteem the words of a religious text, which they called the Bible. An imprecise document, which has been read to me many times these past two hundred and six years, the Bible is replete with teachings that, in the spirit of generosity and not wishing to cause offence, are open to wildly differing interpretations.

Although never explicitly stated, according to the chronology of the Bible, the earth is six thousand years old, give or take the few days it took their God to cobble it all together. Using the Masoretic Hebrew text upon which most translations are based, Adam to Abraham covers two thousand years. Since most agree Abraham lived two thousand years before the time of Christ – if indeed he lived at all – and an additional two thousand years have transpired since, that brings the final tally to approximately six thousand.

How, then, to explain me? Not solely the age of my remains, either. Why did I no longer exist? How could God possibly have allowed one of his creations to become extinct?

These were questions that threatened to undermine the entirety of religious thought. My bones were so vexing that some proclaimed me a fraud, a confection built in the workshop of a heretical madman. They claimed I was little more than *Equus africanus asinus* bones, glued together for dramatic and pecuniary effect. Zealots assumed CW Peale and Thomas Jefferson had conspired in creating the mammoth in order to further their political agenda.

Ironically, the idea of the earth being much older than the Bible claimed had taken root in the writings of Jefferson's rival, le Comte de Buffon. In 1779, the French naturalist posited the planet might be seventy-eight thousand years old. Others took up this notion, and by 1786 it was believed the earth was closer to celebrating its one millionth birthday. Estimates of longevity rose as the years passed and the bones of prehistoric creatures were uncovered. Quite difficult attributing the teeth of a *Tyrannosaurus* to a donkey, as well you must know, *T. bataar*.

When carnivorous donkeys roamed the earth! Terrifying! This ass will eat your ass!

Indeed, *T. bataar*. These days, the hominids believe the planet to be four and a half billion years old, although how they came up with that number is a little beyond me. In any case, it's a tad more than six thousand. But at this time some hominids were willing to question what they knew, or what they thought they knew. As astonishing as it may be to countenance this today, men of science and men of faith were once *the same men*. The world was no longer limited to the church pews of Europe. Explorers sailed forth to map those corners of the globe as yet unknown to so-called civilisation. What they found would challenge their very conception of themselves.

They do say travel broadens the mind. Look at me. I'm just a humble Mongolian boy, living it up in twenty-first-century America. I'm speaking English, shooting the breeze with a dead *Mammut*, talking politics and philosophy and donkeys. I'm about to be sold at auction. Who knows where I'll end up next? It's all so *exciting*.

I thought you found my story tedious.

It has its ups and downs. I mean, no story's gold from beginning to end, right? There's bound to be some boring bits. Although you're killing me with this drip-fed backstory, *Mammut*. Put me out of my misery, will you? What happened after the flood?

You want to go back there already?

Do I ever.

Oh, very well, then. I shall bring that sorry chapter to a close.

Perhaps it was my sheer bulk that saved me, or the odd fondness I developed in my youth for dunking myself into whatever lake I came across on my travels. Proboscidea are excellent swimmers and have been known to cross great bodies of water. We do, after all, possess our very own flexible breathing device.

More likely it was sheer good fortune. When the wave crested, I dove under it and emerged on the other side. I was pummelled by the force of the crashing deluge and struck by several large chunks of ice, but, somehow, I managed to keep my trunk above water. I was swept along for many leagues until eventually I managed to partially drag myself up onto an ice floe. I held fast with my forelegs as the water settled to form an icy inland sea.

My strength was low as I released the flat piece of ice and swam for the new shoreline. By the time I stumbled out of the water, I was exhausted. I lay down on the rocky surface to recover. The sun passed overhead, warming my flanks. I was dimly aware of multiple injuries. Spear wounds. Broken ribs. Internal haemorrhaging. I drifted into a fitful slumber, trying not to think about my son. His chances of survival were nil.

Night fell. The drop in temperature revived me somewhat and I raised my head to listen. An eerie silence rang out across the surface of the newly formed lake. No animals keened or howled at the sky. I had to assume they were all dead, or dying, like I was. I laid my head on the cold earth and quietly mourned the loss of the herd. My friends, my family – all were gone. Was I partially to blame? I could not help feeling that was the case. It was my idea to leave the steppe and head north, my idea to stampede through the Clovis village. The blood on my tusks would never be washed clean.

In the morning I was overcome with a determination to find any survivors. Surely, I could not have been the only one. I struggled to my feet. My back legs were not keen to participate in the effort. I had lost a lot of blood and something was not right in my belly. It hurt to walk, but I did so anyway.

As the sun rose, I looked out across the lake. Hundreds of dead creatures floated on its surface. *Equus* and *Mammut*, mostly, but also Clovis. I skirted the edge of the water, finding more corpses. One or two *Canis dirus*, also. I pushed at their limp bodies with my foot. They fought with savagery and nobility. They gave their all, and for what? They knew the end was coming, that we would probably all perish, and yet they came along anyway, for the pure adventure of it.

There was no sign of any *Mammut* calves. In my heart I knew they were at the bottom of the lake, each and every one.

I searched for hours among the dead until I found him. The *Canis dirus* alpha. His body was battered and bruised. Blood trickled from the gaping wound in his chest. I ran my trunk along his back, stroking the coarse fur.

'Watch what you're doing with that,' he said, his eyes flickering open.

'You're alive,' I said, overcome with relief.

'Not for long,' he rasped. He tried to raise his head but could not. I cradled his jowls with my trunk. 'I was never much of a swimmer.'

'Don't like getting your paws wet,' I said, remembering.

He tried to laugh but coughed blood instead.

'Easy, friend,' I told him.

'We got some of them, huh? You and I, before the flood?'

'We killed many. You were magnificent. I saw you protect a *Mammut* calf. You leapt in front of the knife point.'

'A deal's a deal,' he said, his voice a whisper now.

'He was my son,' I told him.

Canis dirus met my gaze, his blue eyes huge and gleaming. 'I've had a few litters of pups myself. Did he make it?'

I shook my head, unable to answer.

'I'm sorry,' the alpha wolf said.

'Our kind will never forget you,' I told him. 'We owe you a debt.'

'Comforting to know. Except you may be the last.'

'There will be others still walking the steppe,' I said. 'But, yes, our numbers are dwindling. We will survive. We will outlast men; I am sure of it.'

Canis dirus looked up at me wearily. Neither of us believed it. A spasm shook his body and he whimpered in pain. With a supreme effort, he stretched out a trembling foreleg and placed his paw on my foot.

'I hope you find what you were looking for,' he said. 'Now, make it quick.'

'Goodbye, my friend,' I said, resting his head delicately back on the ground.

'See you in the next life, *Mammut*.'

I raised my foot, brought it down on his neck and it was over. My forlorn trumpet call echoed across the face of the waters. I so badly wanted someone to reply, so I might know I was not alone. There was only the fading sound of my grief, and then silence.

The lake was serene in the light of day. It had filled a valley and, were it not for all the floating corpses, a passer-by might easily have assumed the lake had always been there. Nature has a way of exerting a calm dominance over us all. It was beautiful, in a way, how the landscape was changing, becoming something else. The world was moving on. There was no place for the likes of me, or any of our kind. The only slim chance for survival lay to the north, for those who could bypass the many obstacles. I hoped someone else would make it, now I had failed.

There was no point in remaining by the lake. Better to keep going, keep trudging towards the cold mountains I knew lay distant still. My body was racked with shooting pains, but I dismissed them. My muscles were tired, but I ignored the weariness. I walked and kept walking. One foot in front of the other, head down, only looking up to ensure the path ahead was clear.

Hunger clawed at my belly, but I could not eat. I tried taking some couch grass but swallowing it was agony. Something was broken inside me. All I could taste was blood.

I walked for three days and two nights, heading north. Snow began to fall on the morning of the second day. By nightfall the country was cloaked in silken white so clean and pure that had my friend *Canis dirus* been sat atop a rock only his eyes would have been visible.

I was far from the *Mammut* graveyards. It saddened me to know I would not lie with my ancestors. Hunger continued to assail me. Even if I could have digested food, there was none to be had. The snow covered everything.

On the third day, a single *Vulpes lagopus* appeared. She kept her distance, watching me from an outcrop as I lumbered through a forest of denuded trees. She disappeared for a while, and then popped up again ahead of me. I raised my trunk in greeting, but she scampered away. I followed her through the woods. It gave me purpose, however small. Kept me going. Each time I saw her again, she was sitting on her haunches, waiting for me. When finally I neared, she darted away once more into the undergrowth. It was difficult to discern her among the snow. Her fur provided perfect camouflage.

This merry dance continued until darkness shrouded the forest. In order that I might still follow her trail, *Vulpes lagopus* made a series of yips and whispered directions.

'Here,' she said.

'This way.'

'Over here.'

'Not far now.'

In truth, I cannot be certain she was present at all. Exhaustion, hunger and an infection brewing in my spear wounds had made me delirious. I began to stumble through the snow. The little fox waited patiently for me to catch up.

'He's waiting for you,' she said.

'They all are.'

'Your son.'

'Your father.'

'All the *Mammut* that ever lived.'

It was darkest night when, finally, I staggered into a clearing and my legs gave way. I fell headlong into the snow and slid to a halt. It was not an unpleasant sensation. I lay there, letting the soft snow embrace me, staining it with the blood that seeped from the holes in my side. I felt comfortable. Relaxed. At peace.

Vulpes lagopus emerged from the trees and tentatively approached. She sniffed at my foot, and then my trunk. I curled it towards her, and she leapt back.

'I mean you no harm,' I told her. 'Are you even real?'

'That depends,' she said, sitting again on her haunches. 'Do you need me to be real?'

'I suppose it doesn't matter. Why have you brought me here?'

The little fox cocked her head. 'Sometimes we act as guides,' she said. 'For those who are lost. We take them where they need to go.'

'Why here?' I asked. 'Where am I?'

'Look up,' she said, and I did.

The night sky was clear. The light from a million distant suns coruscated down upon me. Did *Mammut* exist on the faraway worlds orbiting those stars? Would my kind live on, elsewhere, out of the reach of man, somewhere in abyssal time? Or was this it? Were we the last?

Green lightning skipped across the darkness. An aurora, which danced in waves of blue, then purple, then red. The sky fizzed and crackled.

'Oh, my,' I said. 'Oh, my.'

And then I died.

Flakes of snow tumbled from the branches of a tree, disturbed by the wind. They fell across my trunk. Soon, I would be covered over. My life had come to an end.

Except not quite. For here you are, *Mammut*. On display in a Manhattan warehouse, telling the saddest story this dinosaur has ever heard.

I am sorry to have upset you, *T. bataar*.

I'm tearing up over here, buddy. You've really tugged the old heartstrings. I'm a tough guy too.

Well, you wanted to hear the rest of the story and there it is. I apologise for the lack of a happy ending, but life is cruel.

It turned out to be a bit of a downer, huh? I can't believe I'm saying this, but I'll be glad to hear you resume the boring old tale of Americans digging up your bones and naming huge cheeses in your honour.

I should warn you, *T. bataar*, there is still some way to go on that story.

At least we'll have some company soon. Looks like they're closing the public viewing. They should be moving some of the other lots in here later.

Perhaps they will provide you with more scintillating conversation.

Tiny fingers crossed!

I thought that was a sensitive subject.

It's okay for a *Tyrannosaurus* to joke about the size of his hands but if anyone else does it's body shaming.

Returning to Philadelphia: my exhibition was not only a success among Joe Public; learned men of wealth and position also attended, although not at the same time as the plebs, of course. Rembrandt Peale, who had quite taken to the role of publicist, organised special evenings. It was during one such soirée that my fate was decided, for I was not doomed to stand forever in a room on the second floor of the Philosophical Society. My travels were only beginning.

Thirteen gentlemen were in attendance that night, representing politics, industry and – although they detest the very notion – American aristocracy. The rich, in other words. They were seated for dinner around a circular table beneath my ribcage. A piano had been installed below my pelvis. A hired musician played such patriotic ditties as 'Yankee Doodle' and 'Jefferson's March' while the men of station dined and quaffed expensive wine. Occasionally one would propose a toast, although Rembrandt had to caution them.

'Take care when raising one's glass, gentlemen,' he said. 'For if you should strike our pet behemoth, it may enrage him.'

I did not appreciate being referred to as a 'pet', but neither did I wish to have my fragile ribs fractured by some corybantic captain of industry. Under the circumstances, I let the insult pass. Not that I was in much of a position to do anything about it.

CW was there too. He was quite drunk on port. Moses had excused himself for the evening in order to avoid the embarrassment of being told he could not attend anyway. As the night wore on, Rembrandt became increasingly alarmed at his father's propensity for boasting, which was given full throat when some fool brought up the French.

'To the American people!' CW raised his glass, spilling some wine on the tablecloth. 'May they be as pre-eminent among the nations of the earth as the canopy we sit beneath surpasses the fabric of the mouse!'

'Hear, hear!' the others cheered, clinking the fancy crystal flutes Moses had recovered from storage earlier that day.

'You refer of course to our august president's *Notes on the State of Virginia*,' one of the industrialists said. Although I paid close attention to all their names, I found it impossible to tell these bewhiskered men apart. 'In which he challenges le Comte de Buffon's assertion that no such beast as the one that looms over us tonight could possibly exist in these territories.'

'Indeed, sir!' CW bellowed. 'Until now we did not possess the ammunition to fight such a battle. Those arrogant French have scoffed at us too long. Once they see the majesty of American nature with their own eyes, they will be both humbled and astounded, I guarantee it!'

'Have you invited any French naturalists to attend your exhibition, Charles?' asked another of the men, a quieter fellow.

'I have, James, and was rudely rebuffed. Ho, wonderful pun not intended! It seems the majority are too busy to examine fresh evidence that might disprove their archaic theories. In truth, I think they consider a trip to the United States to be beneath them.'

'A shame the count passed away before you had a chance to discredit him,' another man said.

'Le Comte de Buffon is dead?' said yet another, quite inebriated.

'Fourteen years ago, you dolt,' his companion replied.

'I was not informed,' the red-faced man said.

'How much have you had to drink, McIntyre?'

'I rather lost track,' he said. 'This is a jolly fine evening, wouldn't you agree?'

'You could present the incognitum to Cuvier,' said the quiet man. 'He would be challenged by it, certainly, but I hear he is more open-minded than his compatriots.'

'Present it to him?' CW said. 'I don't follow.'

'Take the bones to Europe on tour,' the man suggested. 'You're somewhat of a showman, Charles. Make a grand and irresistible presentation to rub their faces in it.'

'I could charge for tickets,' CW said, stroking his beard. 'Although I am exceedingly busy with the museum and my other ventures.'

'Send your boy and his Negro.'

'Now, hold on a minute, Father,' Rembrandt began.

'A capital idea!' CW roared. 'Let's show those Frenchies the true might of America!'

CW raised his glass once more.

'Pack a valise, my boy,' he said to Rembrandt. 'And find some packing cases for our colossus. He is about to become an American ambassador.'

And that, *T. bataar*, is how in the spring of 1802 I ended up on a ship bound for Europe.

I hear it's lovely that time of year.

Would you like me to continue?

Hold your *Equos*, buddy. Here come those notorious archenemies, the mummy and the penguin. Now we're in for it.

Do I have to sit next to him? I don't understand. We have nothing in common. No Egyptian ever set foot on the Antarctic, to my knowledge. Nor would we want to. And no penguin ever swam up the Nile. If he did, he wouldn't last five minutes. One of Sobek's disciples would have him for breakfast. Why do these peasants keep putting us together?

I'm not exactly happy about the arrangement either, Hattie. And who's this Sobek guy?

You blasphemous ingrate. Sobek is the god of fertility. He appears in the form of a crocodile. He is master of impregnation and lord of semen.

Egyptians have a jizz god. Oh, Lordy. Why does this not surprise me?

Penguins have no fertility deity? To whom do you make an offering if you wish to produce offspring?

The great god Pingu. We chant to him in Penguinese: *Neet nit nit nute nit neet nit noot.*

This solemn invocation beseeches the great Pingu to bestow fecundity upon your loins?

Pingu's a stop-motion claymation television show for human children, you idiot.

You are a foul and despicable creature.

We also call upon Mumble, lord of the dance, when we hit the club.

Amun, why am I being punished so? Have I done something to offend thee?

Hey, while you're on the cosmic phone to your god, ask him to make sure we're sold to separate buyers tomorrow, eh?

Do not worry, deformed duck. Even if I am sold, I will surely be reunited with the rest of my form once my provenance is established.

Ooh, ooh, me too!

And who might you be, monster?

Tyrannosaurus bataar, ma'am. I'm from Mongolia. Pretty sure once the feds work it out, I'll be shipped back home.

A swift return to one's homeland is desirable.

Might I inquire who you are, madam? A pharaoh, perhaps?

So she claims.

I am addressing the lady, penguin, not you.

Well, excuse me.

I wouldn't get on the *Mammut*'s bad side, buddy. He'll bore you to death with a lecture on manners.

You are a mammoth?

Indeed, madam. *Mammut americanum*. It seems we find ourselves in a similar predicament.

Sold to the highest bidder, like slaves. The penalty for such impudence should be death. The entrails of those responsible should be thrown to the jackals.

You are a noblewoman, then?

I am Hatshepsut, fifth pharaoh of the Eighteenth Dynasty of Egypt. I ascended to the throne three thousand, four hundred and eighty-five years ago. I ruled as queen and king for two decades until my death.

How did you die, if you do not mind my asking, madam?

Bone cancer, after years of exposure to a carcinogenic skin lotion.

She's full of guano. Don't believe a word of it, guys.

How dare you? The insolence of this aquatic bird knows no bounds.

Oh, come on. I'm *Palaeospheniscus patagonicus*. I've been around ten million years. You don't get to my age and not learn a few things about history.

Dude, I'm never going to get that name right.

My friends call me *Palaeo*.

What, like the diet?

What diet?

The Paleo diet. Vegetables, fruits, nuts, roots and meat.

Wait, there are other kinds of diet?

Let's not get into hominid eating fads. I have no time for nicknames, or the biped tendency to shorten a moniker and then add an 'o' to the end: John-o, Dave-o, Palae-o. Absurd.

I prefer to employ the correct Latin taxonomy.

Sounds like you enjoy showing off, *Mammut*. It's *Palaeo*. I won't answer to anything else.

How wretched. If you insist. You deny this disembodied hand belongs to a female pharaoh, *Palaeo*?

Hatshepsut's body was never recovered, *Mammut*. That tomb robber Howard Carter pulled two female mummies from the Valley of the Kings in 1903, but no-one knows for sure who either of them is.

You are blinded by arrogance, bird. One was my wet nurse Sitre In, and the other was I, Hatshepsut. While it is true I have lain in the tomb these past hundred years, only last month my remains were removed by Dr Zahi Hawass and taken to the Egyptian Museum in Cairo for examination. At this very moment they are matching my body to a molar I mislaid some centuries ago and are about to reveal my identity to the world.

What a story. Every mummy thinks she's a pharaoh. Nobody wants to admit they shovelled horse crap for a living.

Why do you think my hand was severed and stolen? These royal fingers are worth more than all of your peasant limbs combined.

Buyer beware, I say.

Jeez Louise, are you two going to keep this up all night? Have a care, guys. Don't you think I've suffered enough?

There wouldn't be an argument if she only admitted that she's not who she says she is, *T*. You okay if I call you that? *T. bataar* is such a mouthful.

There wouldn't be an argument if this ridiculous animal

would maintain his silence for five minutes.

Allow me to propose a solution. Before you arrived, I was in the throes of telling my friend *T. bataar* here about my recovery from the alluvium. If you like, I can continue. Perhaps you will find it diverting.

Now look what you've done. Thanks, Pingu and Hatshithut.

Hatshepsut, lizard. I have no objection. The *Mammut* seems a noble beast.

As long as she keeps her trap shut.

As long as you both do, friends. I do not care for interruptions. Once a mammoth builds up a head of steam—

Not this again.

I wonder if I should start again from the beginning for our guests.

NO! I mean, no thank you, *Mammut*, that won't be necessary, bro. Pick it up from where you left off, en route to France in the springtime.

A summary of events thus far might at least be in order, *T. bataar*.

Allow me, bud. So, listen, guys, he got killed thirteen thousand years ago after a glacier fell on him, a portrait painter dug him up in 1801, the painter's son and a slave reassembled him with his tusks upside down, none of the bipeds had ever seen the like, he got famous, someone made a cheese in his honour and now he's off to Europe to make America great again. That about sums it up, right, buddy?

I would have elaborated on some points, but yes, I suppose that is more or less correct.

I know you would have. That's why I took the reins. Settle in, kids. We're stuck here all night. Smoke 'em if you got 'em.

The year is 1802. The month is May. We find ourselves midway across the Atlantic Ocean aboard the packet ship *Chimera*. Although the majority of my skeleton is housed within crates stuffed with hay, stowed for safekeeping in the hold of the ship, my skull and tusks have been mounted on a long table in the middle of the saloon. Watching over them are Rembrandt Peale and Moses Williams, two valiant young men tasked with illustrating the true might of America to the indolent French.

It was a risk displaying my head so openly on the boat, and in the midst of a bawdy dining hall to boot. The boys kept a close watch on me through the ventilated doors of their stateroom, which opened out directly into the saloon, should they need to rush forth and deter any overzealous passengers from causing damage to my precious belfry.

The rationale behind such a bold spectacle was thus: since we intended on making a presentation to France's scientific community that would fly in the face of accepted dogma, and the *Chimera* happened to be replete with French merchants wending their way home, it was deemed a sound idea to canvass opinion regarding my existence. A test run, if you like, in order to gauge reaction. In addition, Rembrandt was concerned that my skull and tusks might be damaged in the ship's hold, irrespective of how well they were cushioned. Personally, I was glad to be mounted on the dining table, as such a vantage point enabled me to observe the comings and goings on board the ship. It was my first time sailing, incidentally.

Rembrandt and Moses shared a cabin. These were quite well appointed, albeit cramped. There was room only for a single large mattress, which the boys shared. Fresh linens were supplied every third day. A washbasin provided the means for basic *toilette*. A more fully equipped bathroom lay at the far end of the saloon and was divvied between a dozen staterooms. Although the boys had grown up together and were comfortable coexisting in a state of undress, Rembrandt's mother had packed monogrammed smoking jackets for the men to wear, so they might cover their modesty in front of other paying passengers. Even so, the French did not appreciate the sight of an African wandering past with a towel draped over his shoulder while they breakfasted on croissants and marmalade. There were complaints.

'I don't see what the problem is,' Moses said as he pulled on a pair of long johns one morning. 'Surely I am not so different in appearance from these gentlemen.'

Rembrandt laughed as he dragged himself out of bed, bleary-eyed. 'We may be witnessing the first signs of French inadequacy,' he said. 'This is the purpose of our trip, after all. Although they are supposed to be overawed by the incognitum, not you.'

'They look at me like I'm a field slave and when I talk – the expression on their faces! *Mon Dieu, il parle!* I thought the French were supposed to be enlightened.'

Rembrandt shouldered his friend out of the way, took up the jug of water and poured some into the basin to wash his face. 'I meant to tell you: Napoleon just reinstated slavery in the French colonies.'

'What? When did this happen?'

'Seven days ago. I heard it last night from a man whose brother lives in Guadeloupe.'

'And here I am on my way into the hornet's nest. Impeccable timing.'

Rembrandt and Moses found some allies among the passengers. Americans, on their way to France to conduct business with the new regime. Wrestled away from the stranglehold of the aristocracy, French industry was now in the hands of the proletariat. Napoleon was not yet emperor, although he ruled France as First Consul and regularly conducted plebiscites so the people could help draft policy. In fact, he conducted one only weeks prior to our departure, in which 99.76 per cent of voters approved his appointment as First Consul for life. Half the country abstained from the vote, but the point was moot. Napoleon was in charge. A treaty was signed with Britain, ending the Revolutionary Wars, although the truce would last but a year.

This atmosphere of uncertainty and change proved profitable for the merchant class. There was money up for grabs in France now the rich had been stripped of their assets and, for the most part, their heads. Canny entrepreneurs descended upon the country, seeking investment partners for their business ventures.

One such man was Éleuthère Irénée du Pont, a French American chemist seeking funds to further the interests of his gunpowder company located on the Brandywine Creek in Delaware. Still only thirty years of age, Irénée fell in with my two guardians after a prodigious drinking session in and about my tusks one evening. The fact all three men were bilingual helped forge their association.

'I am *sympa* with your cause, gentlemen,' he told them over a bottle of port. 'America has been kind to my family and provided us with many profitable opportunities. Do not be surprised, however, if my former countrymen treat *la grande bête* as an object of ridicule.' He tapped his glass gently against my tusk. 'Personally, I find it astonishing that a creature of such magnitude once crossed the fields of my family's holdings.'

'There may be more of his ilk buried underfoot,' Rembrandt replied. 'Should you uncover any bones while ploughing a furrow, do let us know.'

'Given the nature of my business, it is more likely they'd be unearthed subsequent to an accidental explosion that dispatches me to my maker.'

'Why gunpowder, Irénée?' Moses inquired.

'It was not my intention to start a business like this,' Irénée said. 'True, I served my apprenticeship in *La Régie des poudres* under Lavoisier, but that was some time ago. The inescapable fact, gentlemen, is that American powder *est de la merde*. Is either of you acquainted with Major de Tousard? He recently opened a military academy with your former President Washington.'

'I am not familiar with the man, though I have heard tell of his exploits,' Rembrandt said.

'He and I were hunting together, and my rifle misfired several times due to the weakness of the powder. Later, when I witnessed the refining process, I realised there was a gap in the market for powder of a higher quality, *et voilà*! I founded my mill in Delaware.'

'I suppose there will never be a shortage of wars to ensure business remains brisk,' Moses said.

'*Exactement,*' Irénée said, raising his glass for a toast. 'May peace never interfere with commerce!'

'Are you men talking of soldiering?'

This inquiry came from a moustachioed biped worse for wear from drink. He was dressed in French military fatigues, although they too had seen better days. He rudely shoved his way onto the bench next to Irénée and placed one arm around the young man's shoulders, out of solidarity. He fixed the American boys with a glassy stare.

'No better man in the field than *un Français*, and I should know, for I am one!' He roared with laughter at this mirthless statement.

'I see from your attire that you have participated in several engagements, monsieur,' Rembrandt said diplomatically.

'One earlier this evening, by the looks of it,' Moses muttered.

'*Tout à fait,* Thierry!' The man's volume assaulted the ears of poor Irénée du Pont, who was a quiet and contemplative hominid. The best kind, in my opinion.

'My name is Rembrandt, but no matter.'

'I fought under Desaix at the Battle of the Pyramids four years ago,' the man barrelled on. 'Twenty thousand of Murad Bey's Mamelukes we slaughtered. The Nile ran red with their blood! Those Egyptian dogs were no match for French ball and steel.'

He lowered his voice then, to a conspiratorial whisper. '*Les sombres* are no kind of soldier. No guile or spirit. *Bien sûr*, they look strong, like your boy here, but faced with European intelligence and bravery, they turn tail and flee, every time.'

'*Comment vous appelez-vous, monsieur?*' Moses asked.

The soldier was taken aback by Moses's question, but he puffed himself up to reply. 'Jean-Pierre Clémentin of Saint Malo, at your service.'

'Good,' Moses said. 'I like to know the names of those I thrash.' He pushed back his chair and stood up. 'Step outside with me, sir, and permit me to demonstrate how "a dark one" fights.'

'Gentlemen, please,' Irénée said. 'Surely there is no need for violence.'

'I beg to differ,' Moses said, tugging on the hem of his coat.

They were set to engage in a bout of fisticuffs when—

Go back for a moment, *Mammut*.

Yes, what is it, Queen Hatshepsut? You have a question?

How rude is she? Didn't you hear the guy say not to interrupt? In future, raise your hand, Princess. Oh, wait.

Silence, bird. Are you saying a battle raged above my tomb, *Mammut*? I didn't hear anything.

Not precisely over your head, madam. Some four hundred miles distant, at Embabeh.

And twenty thousand of our warriors were lost? Is this true?

That is only an estimate. However, it is known the Egyptian army was decimated.

Tell her how many the French lost.

This is no gloating matter, *Palaeo*.

Sure it is. A mere twenty-nine men, Hattie. So, this Clémentin character wasn't wrong in his assessment of Egyptian military nous. In that they don't have any.

I believe none of this.

I'm afraid it's true, madam. Napoleon entered Cairo shortly after and established himself as ruler. Although the victory was short-lived. Within two weeks the British had defeated his fleet on the Nile.

And so, Egypt was returned to the people. Excellent.

Well, if you like. Arguably the struggle for dominance between the Ottoman and British empires ruined your country for the next hundred and twenty years, but let's not delve too deeply into that period for now. On a positive note, the French discovered the Rosetta Stone, which the British appropriated in 1802, the very same year in which my story takes place. It may indeed have been on a ship headed for the British Museum while Rembrandt, Moses and I crossed the seas in the opposite direction. Perhaps we passed it along the way.

Yo, *Mammut*, fill me in, bro. I drifted off there for a minute. Obviously, I know what the Rosetta Stone is and everything, but for the benefit of any fossils in the room that were dug up only recently, perhaps you should explain. Briefly.

Very well, *T. bataar*. The Rosetta Stone is a granodiorite stele—

In lay fossil terms, please.

A slab of igneous rock, upon which is written a decree issued by Ptolemy V. As luck would have it, the text was etched in hieroglyphs, demotic script and Ancient Greek, thus allowing the old Egyptian pictorial language to be translated for the first time. This unlocked the ancient world to modern science, although it took some time for the hominids to work this out.

Educational standards have evidently dropped considerably since my glorious reign.

You will doubtless be pleased to know, madam, that four years ago your friend Zahi Hawass requested the stone be repatriated to your homeland.

Excellent tidings. I assume the foreign devils complied with this demand.

I'm afraid the British Museum has been rather recalcitrant on the subject. A full-scale invasion of their territory might be the only solution.

Then that's what I'll do. As soon as my identity is revealed to the world, I'll be reappointed pharaoh and lead our armies to victory across Europe. It sounds like there are some insults to be redressed.

When are you going to get it through your desiccated skull, lady? You're dead.

I feel very much alive, bird.

Let's not get into this. Take us back to the ship, *Mammut*. I believe you were waving to the passing Rosetta Stone while your hominid companions were bare-knuckle boxing?

Perhaps I have become too concerned with details, *T. bataar.*

I'll say. Skip to the good parts, buddy.

Needless to say, Moses left Monsieur Clémentin in an even sorrier state than he found him. Why hominids insist on fighting when inebriated is a mystery. That is when they have the least control of their faculties. The Frenchman nursed two black eyes and an injured pride for the remainder of the journey, and fewer of his compatriots directed derogatory remarks towards Moses Williams, for fear of humiliation.

In truth, my presentation in the *Chimera* saloon was not a success. To Rembrandt's frustration, the French passengers pointedly ignored my skull, while my tusks were viewed merely as an inconvenience when dining. The American boys were treated as buffoons with ideas above their station, even accused of archaeological fraud. Their protestations fell on deaf ears, while racial epithets were muttered in a francophone hush.

After several weeks afloat, Rembrandt gave up trying to convince the sceptics and passed the rest of the journey reading Wordsworth and Coleridge's *Lyrical Ballads*, a poetry collection that included *The Rime of the Ancyent Marinere*, perhaps not the wisest choice for a lengthy sea journey. A bout of inclement weather in the eastern section of the Atlantic condemned Moses to the privy much of the time. There were no further incidences of pugilism.

Our arrival in Le Havre seven weeks later was greeted with relief from all on board. It was now mid July, and the stiff breezes of the ocean were replaced by a summer heat that had the disembarking passengers tugging at their collars.

Why they bother dressing up so is beyond me. Their ancestors, despite their numerous faults, proved more practical in this regard. A simple cloth to cover the genitalia sufficed, although, again, my question is why bother? They even wear garments while swimming. This makes no sense. Nature provided the hominids with a quick-drying, waterproof skin that is largely bereft of fur. Truly, their denseness baffles me.

When the *Chimera*'s cargo was unloaded onto the dock at Le Havre, I was reunited with my body. My head and tusks were carefully placed into a long wooden crate and stacked with the rest onto three horse-drawn carts. These had been dispatched to Le Havre by our host in France, Jean Léopold Nicolas Frédéric, Baron Cuvier, commonly known as Georges.

Cuvier was France's leading naturalist and a pioneer in the field of palaeontology. He had always been fascinated with fossils and read Buffon's *Histoire Naturelle* over and over as a child. He rose to prominence in Parisian society after recognising the nobleman Henri Alexandre Tessier by chance in the north of France. Tessier was hiding under an assumed name. He had managed to keep his head during The Terror by taking to his heels and, frightened that Cuvier might expose him to the authorities, he provided the young naturalist with an introduction to the highest echelons of the scientific community. His recommendation was thus: 'Gentlemen, I have just found a pearl in the dunghill of Normandy.' High praise, indeed.

Cuvier caused a sensation with his analysis of mammoth fossils like me, for he had some experience with a partial earlier specimen unearthed in Ohio. Having compared the remains to those of African and Indian elephants, Cuvier drew a similar conclusion to Jefferson, much to the consternation of his colleagues. He also wrote a paper on a *Megatherium* found in Paraguay. The publication of his treatise on elephants was published in 1800 as *Mémoires sur les espèces d'éléphants vivants et fossiles.*

This catapulted him into the position of professor at *le Jardin des Plantes*, the foremost botanic gardens in France, and arguably Europe. In short, he was the perfect man to further our cause. All we had to do was reach Paris with my head in one piece. No easy task, given the poor condition of the highways. Fortunately, it had not rained for some weeks, so the heat of the sun had baked the mud dry. Still, it was a bumpy trip from Le Havre. None of the drivers spoke a word of English, so Rembrandt and Moses had an opportunity to relax into the local tongue and work out any rustiness in their diction. I confess to being a little lost at first, but I soon picked up their language, which is quite beautiful. Artful pronunciation seems to lie with the lips, which curl around the words in a kiss. No doubt this is why some hominids think of *le français* as romantic. The language possesses a sensuality lacking in English.

The journey to Paris took several days. During that time, my crate was open to the elements. No rain was expected, and Rembrandt chose to sit on the lip of the box in order to monitor how the ridges in the road might affect my architecture. The bumpiness of the ride was displeasing to Moses, who was still affected by a disorder of the gut from the sea voyage. He chose the most inopportune moments to vomit onto the road, usually when Rembrandt was waxing lyrical on the beauty of the passing landscape.

We stayed at inns along the way. Rembrandt turned a little coin by charging curious locals for the privilege of climbing up onto the cart to view my skull. The sight of me astonished the simple country folk, for they had never witnessed the like. Not one of them questioned the veracity of my existence. They took it as read that if two educated gentlemen were conveying the bones of a long-dead animal all the way from the United States of America to the *Muséum national d'Histoire naturelle* in Paris, there could be no question of deceit. Why would anyone go to such great lengths if this were not an extraordinary find?

I knew we were approaching the city when Moses took to sniffing the air.

'You smell that?' he asked Rembrandt.

'A strong odour of dung and perfume,' Rembrandt agreed.

'Must be Paris,' Moses said.

Le Jardin des Plantes was located in the fifth arrondissement, on the left bank of the Seine. It was a sprawling, rather magnificent place – a curious reminder of French royal opulence. Le Comte de Buffon himself was once curator of the gardens, and they were greatly expanded during his time. A labyrinth was added, for example, a feature that proved extremely popular with coquettish visitors to the gardens. It was the perfect spot for an illicit, if rapid, bout of congress.

Cuvier himself met our troupe when it arrived at the loading dock of the Natural History Museum. The biped was only thirty-two years old, and delighted that Rembrandt and Moses were of his generation. He was a little cool with Moses at first, taken aback by his pallor. He spoke perfect English.

'I was not aware you were of Ethiopian origin, monsieur,' he said to Moses, after salivating over my skull for a few moments.

'Nor was I,' Moses replied tetchily. 'Although it is possible,' he added begrudgingly. 'My lineage is unclear due to poor record keeping. However, I think it matters little, monsieur, for I am American, born and bred.'

'I see,' Cuvier said, a little stiffly. 'Well, permit me to introduce you both to Jacques-Henri Bernardin de Saint-Pierre.'

A much older man stepped forward and bowed theatrically. He was oddly dressed, in a ruffled, open-necked chemise, a high-waisted pair of pants and heavy work boots, all of which were spattered in soil stains.

'Monsieur Saint-Pierre is a well-known author of books for children,' Cuvier continued. 'As well as the manager of these glorious botanical gardens in which we find ourselves.'

'I am pleased to make your acquaintance, gentlemen,' Saint-Pierre said, brushing dirt from his sleeve. 'Please excuse my appearance. I have been planting all morning.'

'We are none too fresh ourselves,' Rembrandt said. 'Having spent several days on the road.'

'May I ask if this beast you convey was a carnivore?' the older man said.

'It was not,' Rembrandt told him. 'We judge from the molars that his species were ruminants, although one wonders if their diet was limited to grass, or if they fed on leaves plucked from the branches of trees using the elongated proboscis.'

Cuvier patted his elder colleague patronisingly on the back.

'Bernardin is an avowed vegetarian,' he explained. 'He believes to devour the flesh of another creature is a sin.'

'Depends on the creature,' Rembrandt said.

'No, monsieur, it does not,' Saint-Pierre said rather haughtily.

Cuvier rolled his eyes. 'Please, Bernardin, let us not have this argument again.' He turned to his guests. 'The French are fond of their meat, gentlemen. Bernardin's views are not widely held in our nation.'

'Some sense to it, though,' Moses said. He affectionately patted one of my tusks. 'Our friend here was likely hunted to extinction for the sake of some steaks to roast over the fire.'

The eyes of both Frenchmen lit up. They nodded furiously.

'This is a most interesting topic, monsieur,' Cuvier said. 'I feel you have come to the right place. Now, I shall have my employees unload this treasure with the greatest of care and bring it to the workshop I have assigned for you during your stay. I am most eager to witness its reconstruction and anticipating the opportunity to study such a magnificent specimen. Unfortunately, I have pressing affairs to attend to this afternoon, but Bernardin will show you to your quarters. Once you are rested, I recommend you take in the air of the gardens. We shall reconvene later this evening for dinner. All the arrangements have been made.'

'Your hospitality is greatly appreciated,' Rembrandt said.

Cuvier bowed and withdrew, leaving the boys in the hands of Bernardin de Saint-Pierre.

'If you would be so kind as to follow me, gentlemen,' he said, indicating they should proceed towards the staff residence behind the museum. 'Our quarters are modest, but I trust you will find everything to your requirements.'

'Tell us more about your career as a writer, monsieur,' Moses said as employees emerged to unload my crates. Fortunately, they took their time, enabling me to bear witness to a most interesting literary discussion.

'I have penned eight works to date,' Bernardin told them. 'Novels and travel narratives, mostly. I spent some time in the West Indies as a youth. My best-known work unfolds on Île-de-France.'

'I have just realised who you are, sir,' Rembrandt said. 'You speak of *Paul et Virginie*.'

The old man's cheeks flushed. He was clearly surprised, delighted and a little embarrassed. 'You have read it?' he asked.

'We both have,' Rembrandt said. He nudged Moses with his elbow. 'Remember the story about the boy and girl in love, and then she perishes in a shipwreck? They stand up to the slave owners?'

Moses clicked his fingers, remembering. 'Yes! We read it when we were boys.' He extended his hand to shake Bernardin's. 'You were a pupil of Rousseau, if I'm not mistaken, and you have argued for emancipation.'

'Correct on both counts,' Bernardin said, enthusiastically clasping Moses's hand. 'You have doubtless heard the First Consul has reinstated slavery in the colonies?'

'During the voyage, yes,' Moses said.

'A despicable state of affairs,' Bernardin said, looking about him. 'But one must be careful of censuring our new despot. He does not respond well to criticism. One is liable to find oneself dead in a ditch, minus one's head.'

'That was a fine book you wrote,' Moses continued, recalling details. 'Rembrandt and I learnt a few tricks from you, monsieur. The way in which your characters calculated the time of day from shadows cast by the trees? We used that frequently.'

'We did, I remember now,' Rembrandt said, smiling at the memory.

'You are too kind,' Bernardin replied. 'The story was performed as an opera ten years ago, but it is no longer running.'

'Why is a famous author working here in the gardens?' Moses asked.

'Come now, gentlemen,' Bernardin said. 'Do not mock me. The income of a writer is paltry and inconsistent. One requires employment that pays a regular salary in order to maintain hearth and home. I am sixty-five years old and have many mouths to feed.'

Moses was crestfallen. Rembrandt patted him on the shoulder.

'He fancies himself a scribe,' Rembrandt explained to their host. 'He writes short humorous tales. They're very good.'

'I have submitted to several newspapers and periodicals,' Moses said. 'As yet, none have responded.'

'Keep trying,' Bernardin told him. 'However, my advice is this: don't give up the day job.'

I'm beginning to see what you mean, *T*.

What? What was that? Sorry, penguin, I was chatting with some of the other new guys. Jeez, it's getting crowded in here. It's going to be a fun night, though. Warehouse party, woot woot!

M really drones on, doesn't he? Loves the sound of his own voice.

He's a stickler for detail, that's for sure. Where's he up to, my little feathered buddy?

Just arrived in France, *T*. Eavesdropping on Moses and Rembrandt's conversation with a French gardener. It's riveting stuff.

He's always stickybeaking on the hominids. Hanging on their every word. It's a bit weird.

I thought the Egyptian was bad, but this guy? Likes to drag a story out, huh?

It could do with a few more sections where he's sitting in his crates twirling his trunk with no hominids around, for sure.

Silence, you curs! Some of us are interested in what the *Mammut* has to say.

Sorry, Your Maj.

Don't apologise to her, *T*. She's just waiting for him to mention the pyramids again. She's a complete narcissist. Typical of these millennials. Three and a half millennia old and she thinks it's all about her.

I swear, when I am reunited with my body, I will command one of my priests to set a curse on you, bird.

Oh, like my life could be worse.

Apologies if my story is interrupting your squabble. You wish me to stop?

Do not pay these ingrates any heed, *Mammut*. I find your tale most soothing. Pray, continue.

Thank you, Queen Hatshepsut. For the sake of brevity, I shall jump forward several days to a dinner party organised by Professor Cuvier for the Americans, so they could present my reconstructed form to his esteemed colleagues of the academy. That should please our Antarctic bezonian.

Don't bet on it.

The soirée in question took place in the Great Hall of the Natural History Museum. It was not a sit-down dinner but instead a mingling affair, where waiters circulated carrying trays of hors d'oeuvres and glasses of champagne. Moses and Rembrandt had pieced me together again for the benefit of the French guests. I stood astride a dais in the centre of the room. It was not a pose of drama or momentum. I looked rather as if I had wandered into the party by mistake and was waiting for someone to take my topcoat.

Cuvier and Bernardin de Saint-Pierre were present, of course, as were academics, scientists, students of natural history, several prominent actresses, a few military men, a politician or two, and a juggler. It is perhaps worth stating for the record that I detest jugglers. I can tolerate the foibles of most hominids, but jugglers should be destroyed. The presence of such buffoonery made a mockery of proceedings, but I suspect that was the intention.

Some openly scoffed at the sight of me, while others begrudgingly expressed their admiration. It was not long before Cuvier found himself engaged in heated discussion over the significance of the elephant in the room.

My apologies. That quip was a little on the trunk. You did say you were bored.

'I have had ample opportunity to examine the fossilised remains that our American friends have made an enormous effort in bringing to France,' Cuvier said to a group of sceptical colleagues as he nervously quaffed champagne. 'And there can be no doubt these are not the bones of a contemporary elephant. This is a quadruped that walked God's Earth many thousands of years ago and is with us no longer. It is extinct.'

'Come now, Georges,' said a smartly dressed man wearing delicate glasses. He appeared to be one of the new breeds of Napoleonic acolytes who formerly occupied positions in the aristocracy and who had been smart enough to see the writing on the wall and reinvent himself as a functionary with standing. 'The notion is absurd. Entire species do not simply vanish from existence. It is against the laws of nature. Just because we have not laid eyes on any of these exaggerated creatures recently does not mean they are all gone. Surely, they still roam free in Africa or the Americas. Perhaps even on the western plains of the new democracy from which our esteemed visitors purport to have discovered the specimen.'

'Our president thinks as much,' Rembrandt told the man, whose name I later learnt was Jean-Marie Dubois, 'since there remain vast areas of terrain as yet unexplored. I do not think it likely, myself. Professor Cuvier's views on this matter of extinction, while they may be controversial, are almost certainly correct.'

'Nonsense,' Dubois snorted, to the merriment of his cronies. 'How is it possible that an animal disappears? Do the buffalo not number in the millions on your continent? Is the mink not abundant? My wife wears a stole fashioned from such a creature's pelt.'

'Exactly, sir,' Moses interrupted. 'What do you think will happen when there are more chilly affluent European necks than furred creatures to keep them warm?'

Dubois rapped my knee bone with his cane. 'Primitive man must have been corpulent in your nation, boy, if he ate all of these.'

The assembled men roared with laughter. Moses's left eye twitched, usually a precursor to someone becoming closely acquainted with his fists.

'Do not listen to them,' Bernardin de Saint-Pierre warned him, scowling at their lack of empathy. 'They are ignoramuses.'

Cuvier ignored the insults. 'Hunting would certainly have reduced their numbers,' he barrelled on, swatting Dubois's cane away from my fragile limb. 'However, after extensive study of ancient fossils such as these, it is my firmly held belief that there existed a world previous to our own, a world without man, ruled by huge, cold-blooded creatures. An age of reptiles, which was destroyed by some catastrophe.'

This theory, while readily accepted by modern bipeds, not to mention every fossil in this room because most of us were there when it happened, was inconceivable to hominids at that time. Virtually no-one other than Cuvier proposed such madness. His determination to promote the idea that beasts such as I, or you, *T. bataar*, once held dominion over the world, until we were swept away by tsunami, earthquake and asteroid strikes, was a source of embarrassment to his colleagues. When he died in 1832, the scientific community breathed a sigh of relief and quickly reverted to uniformitarianism as an explanation.

The focus of ridicule thus shifted from me, standing there like a lost calf, to Cuvier, the founder of vertebrate palaeontology and author of *La Règne Animal*, the first biped to correctly speculate as to the fate of all our kind.

'Preposterous.'

'Tantamount to blasphemy.'

'The only catastrophe is that you were granted a professorship, Cuvier.'

'An age of reptiles? Is this your thinly veiled critique of the monarchy, Georges? Our dearly departed Dauphin may have somewhat resembled a toad, but I had not realised you were such an ardent republican.'

Cuvier remained impressively impassive, for he was inured to such criticism, having heard it all many times before. Rembrandt and Moses were not so easily mollified.

'The disrespect you show such a great man of science is deplorable, gentlemen,' Rembrandt interceded. 'Are your minds so closed to possibility that you cannot countenance a theory of the world that is different from your own? How can you be so sure what you believe is correct?'

Moses waggled his forefinger in the faces of the assembled sceptics. 'Increasing numbers of large fossils indicate that history may not be what we think. Only a fool would dismiss the evidence presented here tonight before your very eyes. Gaze upon the incognitum, gentlemen, and tell me with hand on heart that we are not entering a period of profound scientific change.'

That Moses addressed them so eloquently was clearly a source of irritation to Dubois and his cabal. Dubois poked Moses in the chest with the tip of his cane.

'You forget your place, boy,' he said.

Moses snatched the cane from the man's grasp and broke it in twain over his knee.

'How dare you,' Dubois said, unbuttoning his jacket as if preparing for a bout of fisticuffs.

Cuvier stepped between the two cockerels. 'Gentlemen, please. I implore you. Let us not ruin the party with base violence. Surely we can hold differences of opinion without resorting to blows?'

Dubois stretched his neck and brushed himself down. '*Ces Américains sont des têtes chaudes,*' he said, laughing as if the snapping of his cane was no matter of consequence, when clearly he was furious.

'*Et pourtant nous avons du sang froid,*' Moses replied.

'I advise caution, monsieur,' Rembrandt said. 'My brother's facility with languages is only matched by his irascibility. He was also the best boxer in our school.'

Dubois snorted, and then bowed. 'I am more of a fencing aficionado, myself.'

'Doesn't surprise me,' Moses said, handing him back the pieces of his cane. 'I will pay to have your walking stick replaced, monsieur, on the proviso you stop poking people with it.'

'I do not require it to walk. It is a mere affectation.'

'That doesn't surprise me either,' Moses said.

'Professor, tell us more about the catastrophe scenarios of which you speak,' Rembrandt said, bringing the discussion back to safe ground.

'Yes, do tell,' Dubois added. 'Illuminate us as to how your giant reptiles were eradicated, so we may prepare in case of their return.'

'I have exhaustively researched accounts in Greek and Latin from the ancient world relating to the discovery of large bones petrified in rock,' Cuvier began. 'There are several distinct possibilities regarding the nature of the catastrophe, or series of catastrophes, that befell our world, mostly relating to the Biblical notion of a great flood. The Swiss geologist Jean-André Deluc held that ten thousand years ago the continents collapsed, and the ocean floor rose to the surface. Thusly, all animal life was ravaged. If that seems unlikely to you, consider the theory of Déodat de Dolomieu, who postulated that a tsunami circled the globe with the same result. Either way, something dire happened that changed the face of our world.'

'How was such a wave caused, Georges?' Dubois asked. 'And should I inform my children to avoid the beach this summer?'

'A seismic event on the ocean floor, perhaps,' Cuvier replied, ignoring the barb. 'Or, if a rock of significant size were to fall from the heavens and strike the sea at sufficient velocity, a tsunami would occur.'

'When pieces start breaking off the moon and tumbling to Earth, be sure to let me know, Georges.'

Asteroids! He's talking about asteroids! What did I tell you, bro? One could hit us at any minute.

Let's not be alarmist, *T. bataar*.

To what is the great lizard referring?

Our friend witnessed an apocalyptic event some sixty-six million years ago, Queen Hatshepsut. It has rather stayed with him.

A huge rock from the sky, Your Maj! Slammed into the planet – BAM! – and that was the end of everything for a while. I'm lucky to be standing here.

It came from the heavens? From the stars?

I don't know where else it could have come from.

A punishment from the gods, then, *Tyrannosaurus*.

Could be, could be. Except we didn't have any gods in my day.

That does not mean they weren't there, watching.

I kind of like the idea of a *Tyrannosaurus* god. Though she'd hardly be lenient or forgiving. More the vengeful type, I reckon.

We have many gods, monster. They serve a variety of purposes. I worshipped Amun, the invisible one.

I heard a crazy story that your so-called gods were actually from the stars, Hattie.

I wish you would not call me that, bird. I am Hatshepsut, fifth pharaoh of the Eighteenth Dynasty—

Yeah, yeah, keep telling yourself that.

What is this deception of which you speak, penguin?

I'm saying your civilisation was built with assistance from beings – bipeds, most likely, though not like this lot – who hailed from another world, somewhere up there among the stars.

I have also heard this theory, *Palaeo*. I dismissed it as frivolous.

Why do you think this, bird?

Your technology seemed awfully advanced for its day, Hattie.

That is not remarkable. We have always been a clever people.

What about the pyramids, eh? Who built them?

Slaves.

Really? No help from little green men?

Some of them turned green with disease and exhaustion, but we cast those ones into a pit. Others took their place.

Seems a tad unlikely, Hattie.

Not at all. When one is the absolute ruler of a vast nation – as I was – one can do what one likes. Tens of thousands of slaves worked on the tombs day and night. Egypt was a constant construction site, which was irritating on occasion. You know how subcontractors can be. Agitators, every one. They would have held up proceedings interminably, had I not ordered their throats slit.

Entrails fed to the jackals, I'm guessing?

Naturally, penguin. What else does one do with entrails?

Best-fed jackals in the world, seems like. So, none of these 'gods' ever popped down for a visit, to see how it was all going?

I am sure they did, bird, but I was not personally blessed with a visitation from Amun. However, rocks did fall from the sky into the desert on occasion. A loyal vassal gifted one to me. Its colouration was strange.

Admittedly, I've seen them too. Not a planet-changing asteroid like yours, *T*, but some decent-sized meteors crashing into the sea.

What did I tell you, *Mammut*? They're coming down all the time! I'd be surprised if we make it through the night.

I think we'll be fine. Tell me, *Palaeo*, did these meteors cause tidal waves as Cuvier postulated?

I've seen a few, yeah.

Would you care to elaborate?

Oh, now you want to hear the penguin's tale.

Yes, yes! Come on, little buddy, tell us about your adventures on the high seas. I don't think I can stand much more of Frenchmen arguing. No offence, *Mammut*.

It is all right, *T. bataar*. I shall not tarry in France much longer.

It used to be quite nice in the Antarctic, back in the day. I'm talking about way back, you understand. Before the hominids turned up in their creaky sailing ships and planted flags on the ice. I lived on an island. It was cold and dry there, and the fish were plentiful. You would have liked it, *M*. Not much vegetation, though. The island's gone now. Sunk beneath the waves. Destroyed, just like your Frenchman said, by earthquakes. It was called Tsalal.

You spent your whole life there, bird?

Thank you for finally showing an interest, Hattie.

I am not uninterested in your experiences, penguin. It is merely that I find you annoying.

That's about as close as you've come to complimenting me.

It was not intended as such.

To answer your question, yes. I lived on Tsalal until I died. Mine was a contented, uneventful existence. I swam in the great Southern Ocean, I protected the eggs of my brood during storms, and I consumed vast amounts of krill. Squid on Sundays. The world was a simple, elemental place. My sole concern was not being eaten by *Hydrurga leptonyx*. Those bastard leopard seals are number two on the Antarctic food chain and, boy, do they know it. They took friends, family and children of mine. Not an ounce of mercy in their whiskers.

Who is number one?

Orcinus orca, Hattie. What a joy it is to witness a pod of *orca* working together to knock one of those dumb seals from its perch. You asked if penguins had gods, Hattie? *Orca* is as close as it gets, except they're alive. Some of the bipeds believe *orca* take on hominid form under the waves and live in houses on the ocean floor. Others think they rule an undersea kingdom, keeping seals as slaves.

I have heard it spoken on the eastern steppe that *Orcinus orca* transforms into *Canis lupus* during winter and that the Yupik cast tobacco into the sea as an offering.

Ah, the humans have funny customs, *M*.

How did you die, bird?

Hydrurga leptonyx got me in the end, Hattie. I was getting old and slow. One of them took a chunk out of me, but I managed to escape by leaping out onto the ice and sliding into a crevasse. He followed me but couldn't work his snout down in there. I retreated far into the crevasse and became trapped. Died from my wound, eventually. The ice froze around me, and I was encased for years. Then the years turned to centuries, and the centuries to millennia. Thankfully my spirit had gone to the happy hunting grounds, otherwise that would have been a nightmare.

You were not aware, as you are now, *Palaeo*?

No, sir. Dead and gone, or so I believed. It wasn't until 1836 that I found myself back in the land of the living, or whatever you guys are calling this plane of existence.

Fossilife!

Very good, *T. bataar*, except it sounds like a hominid dietary supplement.

Want to lose weight fast? Throw off that flesh and sinew with new Fossilife! Guaranteed results, or your money back!

Tsalal was still around in 1836, and it even had some biped inhabitants. Their skin was dark like that of your friend Moses. They were afraid of the colour white. If they saw it, they would cry out in the old tongue.

Tekeli-li?

Exactly, *T.*

I have some questions, *Palaeo.*

Fire away, *M.*

How did hominids such as these come to live on your island? Surely it is distant from Africa?

Not as far as you'd think. Search me, though. I'm guessing they rowed directly south. Maybe got lost or were carried to the island in a storm. Next question.

Fear of the colour white must have been a severe disadvantage in a polar environment. How did they cope?

Not sure how this happened, *M*, but by the time I was blasted out of the rock, the ice on Tsalal had melted. The weather had turned quite balmy.

Blasted?

Yes. Some accursed sailors from the north turned up in their tall ship and got into a beef with the locals. There I was, minding my own beeswax, locked in the side of a hill, when KA-BLAMMO! An explosion of some kind brought half the mountain down on the heads of explorers and locals alike. Most were killed, though a few sailors escaped in a stolen pirogue. I only know this because I found myself exposed to the elements again, wondering what the hell was going on. Lucky, some might say, for Tsalal sank a few years later.

You did not sink with the island, I presume.

Nope. There was another survivor, an Irishman called Domhnall. He was injured in the landslide and left for dead but nursed himself back to health during the subsequent months. Took quite a shine to me, after he found my bones petrified in rock. Talked to me at nights. That's how I learnt English. Poor lad. He was very lonely and terrified he might never be rescued. Good sense of humour, though. Made the most of being shipwrecked, with only a ten-million-year-old fossilised penguin for company.

How long were you stranded with this Irishman, bird?

It was eighteen months before another ship sailed into the bay. They'd come looking for their missing comrades from the north. Domhnall was pleased to see them, though his account of what had occurred was a disjointed ramble. The new sailors could make little sense of it, for they thought him mad, clutching a penguin encased in rock to his chest. They picked him up, in any case, and after a sightseeing tour of the Antarctic – which I didn't mind at all, after being away for so long – they turned around and sailed back to Patagonia. My namesake, you know. From there, Domhnall secured passage on a ship travelling up the east coast of South America. A shame he couldn't have zipped along the other side – I would have liked to visit Peru.

My ancestor *Icadyptes salasi* hails from there. Now that was a penguin! As big as a hominid and with a beak five times the length of my own, *Icadyptes* was an apex fisherman. Bit slow on his feet and fond of sunbathing – not a glacier man like me – but still, he'd give those leopard seals a run for their money, of that I'm certain.

I rather enjoyed my voyages with Domhnall. Admittedly, he wasn't the brightest egg in the clutch. The hominid equivalent to plankton. Not much going on in that soft skull of his. He floated from one place to another without rhyme or reason, not caring where the winds carried him. But he had a good heart. It was thanks to him I wound up in Boston. Likely our adventures would have continued from there, but the poor lad had the misfortune of winning at dice one fateful night and took a blade between the ribs for his trouble. He bled to death in the street out the back of Faneuil Hall.

The landlord of the dosshouse where he flopped had no forwarding address for his relatives, so he sold off Domhnall's possessions, me included. I was purchased by a local tavern owner and mounted above the bar. Ownership of the pub changed hands many times down the years, but I always remained. The joint was even named after me for a while: The Penguin. That's where I've been for the past century and a half. Man, the things I've seen. I don't even want to think about it.

Why then are you here for sale, *Palaeo*?

The place closed down six months ago. Money troubles. I tell you what, there's a crisis brewing. Mark my words. We better hope to get situated before the recession hits. Nobody's going to be spending up big on fossils this time next year, friends.

I would not concern yourself too much. I am sure a fossil of your age and pedigree will be snapped up by a museum.

Honestly, *M*? I fucking hope not. Send me back to the wall of a pub somewhere. That's where the action is.

There is no need to swear, *Palaeo*.

I've been living in Boston for one hundred and sixty-seven years. Give me a frigging break over here.

Interesting that you should encounter an Irishman. My own *Mammut* tale is intertwined with that particular race of hominid.

Some of my best friends are Irish. Well, Irish American. Pretty sure they're more into Ireland than anyone who lives there. I've heard it's actually a bit of a shithole. Green, rolling hills and all that, but a sodding-wet nation of alcoholic misanthropes.

I shall tell the story and you can be the judge. Fair warning to you all, I am about to resume my tale approximately half an hour after I left off.

Still at the dinner party? Oh, come on, *Mammut*!

Never fear, *T. bataar*. We are on the home straight.

Ruffled and disappointed by the contemptuous reaction from the French scientific community, Rembrandt and Moses ate their *foie gras* canapés and attempted to drink as much of the free champagne as possible. Dubois periodically introduced them to more of his sneering colleagues, simply to put the Americans through the humiliation of justifying my existence all over again. After the latest round of derision, Moses excused himself and retired to the balcony for some fresh air. Since the hominid conversation within the hall was so tedious and dismissive of my grand form, I cocked a phantom ear in the direction of the balcony, so I might follow a more engaging strand of conversation. Mammoth have huge ears and excellent auditory capacity, even when dead.

Bernardin de Saint-Pierre was there, conversing with a sternly dressed man and a young woman whose evening attire spoke of a practical, rather than a glamorous, mien. She adjusted the blue silk band at her waist, which was worn uncomfortably high. The dress was white and had a short bustle and train. The lady wore no make-up, as was the choice of the times.

'Ah, Monsieur Williams,' Bernardin called out to him. 'You have come to take the air?'

'It's a little stale in there for my liking,' Moses said.

'Permit me to introduce you to two other visitors from abroad. This is Monsieur Robert Emmet and Mademoiselle Caoimhe O'Neill. They are from Ireland.'

Emmet bowed curtly. Miss O'Neill offered her gloved hand. Moses touched it to his lips.

'That is a pleasant name,' he said. 'I have not heard it before.'

'Try spelling it,' Miss O'Neill said.

'I would not dare. I am Moses Williams, one of the foolish Americans you have no doubt heard disparaged this evening.'

'We know who you are,' Emmet said.

'I tend to stand out in such company,' Moses said. 'Tell me, have you been wed this evening, Miss O'Neill?'

Caoimhe hoisted the waistband of her dress once more. 'I don't blame you for thinking so. Apparently, the current style is for a lady to dress like a statue come to life, or a bride about to take her vows.'

'Is it?' Moses said, chuckling. 'I know nothing of such matters, I'm afraid. I must look like a peasant to these gentlemen of learning.'

'You are dressed entirely appropriately, Moses,' Bernardin told him. 'In fact, some of the men present tonight take a risk with their opulent outfits. It is considered poor taste to dress like an aristocrat these days. Dangerous, even.'

'Plain is in,' Emmet said, slapping Moses on the arm. 'Just as well for us, eh?'

'Meantime us girls have to dress like we're for sale,' Caoimhe said. 'I feel like a street *hoor* in this get-up.'

'Caoimhe,' Emmet cautioned her. 'This is not Dublin. We're in polite company now.'

'I wouldn't go that far,' Moses said. 'Are you aware, miss, that when the candlelight shines upon you, your gown becomes transparent?'

'You noticed that, did you?'

'It is hard not to. I felt compelled to point it out.'

'We live in the age of undress, sir,' she told him. 'Nudity *à la grecque*, it's called. Rest assured, this is the first and last time I wear such a foolish outfit. I can barely breathe.'

'Sniff some of your potion, Caoimhe,' Emmet said. 'Before you pass out.'

The Irishwoman opened the reticule she carried and took out a small flask. She unscrewed the top and inhaled its contents.

'Oh, that's good stuff,' she said.

'May I?' Moses asked.

'On your own head be it,' she told him, offering the bottle.

Moses took a cautious sniff and reeled from the noxious odour. 'God Almighty. What is that?'

'Spirit of hartshorn,' Caoimhe said. 'A distillation of ammonia from the shavings of deer horn.'

'That's more potent than the booze they're serving,' Moses said.

'I can sell you some, if you like,' Caoimhe said. As she put the flask away, Moses caught a glimpse of a tiny handgun nestled in her bag. Miss O'Neill noticed that he had observed the weapon.

'A muff pistol,' she told him. 'It's a .42 calibre. Not enough to penetrate heavy clothing but if I shot you in the head, it might smart a little.'

'May I inquire as to why you carry it?'

'Personal protection,' she said. 'Who knows what desires these so-called gentlemen harbour? Especially when they can see right through my fecking dress.'

Moses held up his hands as if being robbed. 'Am I to regret raising the matter of the pellucid garment?'

'You're all right,' she told him. 'I'll just stand in the shadows where I belong. That should do the trick.'

'Are you also armed?' Moses asked Emmet.

'Always,' the Irishman said. 'Are you not? I thought you were American. Is it not enshrined in your constitution?'

'It is, but I didn't expect to engage in a gunfight at the *Muséum national d'Histoire naturelle*.'

'It's still early,' Caoimhe said.

'Mademoiselle O'Neill and Monsieur Emmet are attempting to secure funds for another rebellion in Ireland,' Bernardin interjected.

'We wish to shuck the yoke of English tyranny,' Emmet said. 'Much as you have done in the Americas. We are also inspired by the revolution here in France, of course.' He bowed to Bernardin, who acknowledged the gesture with a polite smile.

'There are plenty of wealthy men here tonight,' Moses said. 'A good opportunity to secure a patron or two, I'd have thought. I doubt you'll encounter many defenders of the English.'

'Hence the diaphanous gown,' Caoimhe said. 'We must be desperate, if it's come to this.' She fussed with her black ringlets.

'I'm not usually one to judge by appearances,' Moses said. 'So please forgive my impertinence, but you do not look particularly Irish, mademoiselle.'

Caoimhe held out her tanned forearms for inspection. 'I've been sunning myself in the gardens. I prefer the outdoors life.'

'Are you one of those Celts who inherited Spanish blood, from when the Armada foundered on your shores?' Moses asked. 'I heard shipwrecked sailors were harboured by locals, in contravention of the English decree that they be surrendered for execution.'

'It's possible but unlikely. That tale's a bit of a myth. Most people did as they were bade and handed the Spanish over to the garrisons. Some six thousand men were put to death as a result.'

'Surely there must have been some sympathisers.'

'They reckon maybe a hundred men got away, although when Philip II sent an envoy to look for them, only eight fellers turned up.'

'If anyone helped the Spaniards, it would have been the O'Neills,' Emmet said with confidence. 'If only to annoy the English.'

'There were rumours,' Caoimhe admitted. 'I never held much truck by that talk. If it's true, I appreciate the bloodline, right enough. Unlike most, I can work out under the sun without bursting into flames.'

'A useful skill,' Moses said. 'I have known Irish whose skin turns so red with the sun that they could easily be mistaken for the natives in my country.'

'Their skin is not red, surely?' Bernardin asked.

'No, I shouldn't say that,' Moses apologised. 'It's pejorative, and incorrect.'

'You know Georges keeps an archive of American Indian observations and legends surrounding skeletal remains? It is from these people that he has developed his theory of giants once walking the earth.'

'I was not aware,' Moses said. 'I should ask him about that.'

'I shall fetch him for you, Moses. He will likely appreciate a break from his guests.'

'We should come with you,' Emmet said, taking Caoimhe by the arm. 'We're not raising any money standing out here admiring the view.'

'Perhaps we can talk further later, Mr Williams?' Caoimhe said.

'I would enjoy that very much. My brother and I are staying here in one of the staff cottages. Come and visit tomorrow, and we shall have lunch together in the gardens.'

'Best offer I've had all week,' Caoimhe said.

With that, the Irish duo took their leave, heading back into the room in search of a sympathetic ear. Alone for a moment, Moses peered out over the balcony into the gardens. Gas lamps illuminated the pathways through the foliage. Several couples strolled by, enjoying the warm evening.

The peace was broken by the arrival of Cuvier and Dubois, in the midst of a heated exchange. They halted their argument to greet Moses.

'Bernardin tells me you have been discussing the American Indian,' Cuvier said to Moses.

'In passing,' Moses replied. 'One of your fascinations, I believe?'

'This is the problem with you, Georges,' Dubois said. 'Your theories are based on the hearsay of heathens. Don't you know this undermines your scientific authority?'

'What do you know of the American native, monsieur?' Moses said, irritated all over again by the demeanour of the abrasive Frenchman, who seemed to revel in his obstinacy.

'Only what de Pauw and Buffon say,' Dubois said, stiffening. 'That they are as degenerate as everything else on your continent. I hear the Indian males have genitalia so insignificant, they are practically eunuchs. That milk squirts from their breast. That men and women alike are riddled with venereal disease. Also, they are lazy beyond comprehension. Where are their crops, for instance? Their hatred of labour never induced them to cultivate the earth. They have no compassion for their elders, leaving them to perish when they no longer serve a purpose. They are incapable of forethought, lack any nobility of mind and are useless to themselves and to society. A direct consequence of living in the miserable climate of your nation, monsieur.'

'Quoting Cornelius de Pauw verbatim does nothing to prove your point, Monsieur Dubois,' Moses said, keeping his cool. 'The man never left Europe. He believed the Esquimaux licked their newborns clean like dogs, for goodness sake, and that Indian mothers kneaded the soft heads of their infants into a conical shape. Such ludicrous theories have been utterly discredited.'

Dubois scoffed at Moses's rebuttal. 'This is a rich opinion, coming from an Ethiopian.'

'All right, I've had enough of that. *Quelle est cette merde sur les Éthiopiens?*'

Despite their opposing views on fossils and Native American lore, Dubois and Cuvier were united in their belief that hominids could be classified into three distinct groups. It was in fact Cuvier who proposed this theory of scientific racism, which became entrenched in western society for many years to come.

Cuvier was a little embarrassed to be confronted in such a manner.

'You called me that before,' Moses said to him. 'What are you talking about?'

Cuvier cleared his throat. Dubois adopted a louche grin. He knew what was coming.

'My studies show there are three distinct races of man. Caucasian, Mongolian and Ethiopian – white, yellow and black. As progenitors of the original race, Adam and Eve were of course Caucasian. When the world was upended by catastrophe, survivors scattered to the four winds. From that point on, the

Mongolian and Ethiopian peoples lived in isolation from the master race.'

'The what?' Moses said, astonished to hear such a theory expounded by a naturalist he otherwise admired.

'Well, the white race, with oval face, straight hair and nose, to which the civilised people of Europe belong, and which appear to us the most beautiful of all, is superior to the others by its genius, courage and activity,' Cuvier explained.

'Is that so?' Moses said. 'And the Ethiopian?'

'Characterised by its black complexion, crisp woolly hair, compressed cranium and flat nose. The projection of the lower parts of the face, and the thick lips, evidently approximate it to the monkey tribe. The hordes of which it consists have always remained in the most complete state of barbarism.'

'Tell me something, Professor,' Moses said. 'How is it that you can be so progressive in regard to the evolution of animals, yet so backward when it comes to humans?'

'I am not sure I follow.'

'How do you explain someone like me?'

'That's easy,' Dubois said, patting Moses on the shoulder. 'Even a monkey can be trained to play the cymbals.'

'Take your hands off me, sir, or I'll play your cymbal.'

'Ah.' Dubois beamed. 'It shows its true colours. They are naturally aggressive, don't you find, Georges?'

Moses forced himself to remain calm. 'You deny to my face that I am a man of education and wit?'

'A mere parlour trick,' Dubois said. 'No doubt you are parroting the badinage of a more elevated Caucasian. Perhaps your master,

Charles Peale. It is an accomplished act of mimicry, nothing more. None of what you say actually registers in your brain. It is too small to accommodate complex notions.'

Moses laughed. He could do little else. 'Would you have me solve a mathematical equation for you, or annotate an opera, by way of demonstration? Surely neither of you actually believes this?'

'Admittedly, you are a vexatious case,' Cuvier said. 'Perhaps explained by your environment. You were raised by Caucasians and have never lived in Africa; therefore, you have become more Caucasian. Have you noticed a lightening of your skin over time, Moses?'

'How is that possible?'

'You were once of the same race as us, many thousands of years ago. Increased brain function might be an indication of reversion. I would love to examine your cerebellum,' Cuvier said. Then hastily added, 'Once you are dead, of course.'

'Very considerate of you to wait,' Moses said. 'I shall be sure to remember you in my will.'

'Skin colour is a result of climate,' Dubois announced. 'You have noticed how the Irishwoman's arms have turned golden in the sun? I met her earlier. A delightful creature, if a little coarse. The Ethiopian is dark-skinned merely because it lives in a hot area of the earth. If it were moved to the northern climates and lived there for several hundred years, perhaps fewer, its skin would turn white.'

'Clearly, you have not been to Philadelphia. It is often akin to living in the Arctic.' Moses snatched another glass of champagne from a passing tray, held aloft by a waiter. 'Gentlemen, this is an old argument, and a tiresome one. It is obvious that even if I proved Fermat's Last Theorem while standing on one leg and whistling "Adams and Liberty", you would still view me as inferior. If you will excuse me, I am going to seek civilised conversation elsewhere.'

Jeez, they were rough on that kid.

Indeed they were, *T. bataar*. Moses was correct to point out the senescence of the argument. Le Comte de Buffon had proposed a similar experiment some years prior, when he suggested that a group of people from Senegal should be transported to Denmark. Once installed in the country of white-skinned, blue-eyed and golden-locked northerners, the Senegalese would be kept separate from the Danes, in order to prevent cross-contamination of bloodlines. 'This is the only method of discovering the time necessary to change a Negro into a White, or a White into a Black, by the mere operation of climate,' Buffon claimed. Future generations would, he believed, report that all pigmentation had faded from the skin of the Senegalese, rendering them virtually indistinguishable from their bemused Danish hosts.

Moses was also right when he pointed out the dichotomy of Cuvier's contributions to science. For a man whose work led to the coining of the term 'dinosaur', a man who had animals and an island named after him, a man whose name is one of seventy-two that adorn the Eiffel Tower, Cuvier had an archaic attitude towards race. A sad postscript to the scientist's longstanding legacy is that racial stereotypes have been perpetuated in hominid culture ever since the foolish biped came up with them. Honestly, friends, I do not know what goes through their tiny skulls sometimes. Incidentally, it may interest you to know, madam, that after Napoleon's campaign in your nation, men of science such as Monsieur Cuvier decreed that Egyptians must have originally been Caucasian.

Why would they think so?

How could the pyramids have been built, otherwise? That was their question.

How many times do I have to say this: slaves! How else are you supposed to create infrastructure?

They did not mean construction in a practical sense, madam.

I understand what they meant. The truth is, my people were great architects while they were still wallowing in the mud. That wooden-faced son of an adulterous whore Cuvier can go to sixty thousand hells.

I don't mean to be rude, *Mammut*, but you said you were winding this up, and that was about an hour ago.

Only moments ago, surely, *T. bataar*. Don't exaggerate.

It feels like an hour.

Very well, then. I shall accelerate.

Moses was somewhat glum after the party, for it seemed the likelihood of my existence stood a fractionally greater possibility of being accepted than his own, and I had been dead for over ten thousand years. The temporary exhibition was opened to the public for a brief time, minus the fanfare CW had whipped up in Philadelphia. Citizens came to gawk and jeer and shake their heads. Everyone wanted to argue with the Americans. Moses soon tired of such disputes, especially given how often the discussion needlessly turned to his own genetics. He left Rembrandt to contend with the vagaries of French pseudo-intellectualism and frequently retired to the cottage, or found a quiet spot in the gardens, where he could read in peace.

The boy came to visit me in the evenings after the exhibition was closed and the public had departed. Despite a prominent sign that read: *FRAGILE – NE PAS TOUCHER*, visitors could not keep their grubby mitts to themselves. My legs and tusks were often quite dirty by the end of the day. Moses – bless the lad – cleaned the stains from my ivory with a chamois cloth and a mild soap solution. When no-one was around, he talked to me too, revealing his fears and concerns. It was all rather confessional.

'I must apologise for this, Incognitum. I've apprised Bernardin and Professor Cuvier several times about this sorry situation. They promised to assign guards to prevent people from touching you, but, alas, the men they send are hopeless. They're either asleep on that chair in the corner or can be found smoking their pipes with their confederates out by the loading dock. One even misunderstood the instructions completely – wilfully, in my opinion – by encouraging visitors to place their hands on you. Short of stationing myself by your side all day, I cannot prevent this violation. And I am reluctant to do that for fear of drawing further ridicule. They view us as a travelling freak show, it seems. The Ethiopian and the Mammoth. We are two clowns for their amusement.

I do not know if either of us will achieve acceptance in this lifetime. That probably bothers you less than it does me. No-one will disinter my carcass ten millennia from now to marvel at my form. In fact, no-one will be able to tell the difference between my bones and those of the so-called Caucasians. Death reduces all men to their composite parts. Skull, spinal column, ribs, pelvis and limbs. The dead are unremarkably similar. The colour of the skin that once covered their bones is inconsequential. But you, big fellow? I wonder how many more of your kind there are buried around the world, and if there are other ancient creatures we are yet to discover. Cuvier may be an irritating dogmatist, but I suspect he has stumbled upon a great truth concerning our past. An age of reptiles! What a marvellous notion. I hope it is proven correct. I would give anything to be able to travel back to that period and see it with my own eyes. I probably wouldn't survive very long, true, but it would be worth it. I fear I was born in the wrong time.

'Bernardin aside, the only others in this place who are content to converse with me as an equal are the Irish. They have told me much about their struggle for independence from their oppressors, and I feel a kinship with their cause. They are slaves too, after a fashion. Perhaps I would fare better on their island, were I free to travel there without consequence. Although they inform me that I would be even more of a curiosity in Ireland than I am here or back home. Perhaps one day a man of colour may parade freely in the street without fear of aggression or condescension. That does not seem too much to ask, Incognitum, and yet...

'I confess there is another reason I am drawn to the Celts. You may have guessed by now that I have been spending many of my afternoons in the company of Caoimhe. My apologies, I mean Miss O'Neill. She is indeed a remarkable woman of great fortitude and ample, uh, charms. She possesses a razor-sharp wit and makes me laugh ceaselessly. We have explored the park in all its beauty, and ventured beyond, into the streets of Paris. Certainly, we have gathered stares of disapproval but also some of envy. She has no compunction in taking my arm, sees nothing wrong with presenting me to society as her beau. Nor should she, of course, but these are strange times in which we live. She risks censure, perhaps, and I have heard passers-by mutter hurtful whispers, but Caoimhe does not care and I love her for that.

'Well. Love is a strong term, which should not be employed casually, Incognitum. I wonder if you ever knew love, if the stirrings of indelible attraction caused tumult in your soul. I do not love Miss O'Neill per se, nor am I in love with her. That seems an extreme reaction to our brief time together. But I love what we have. Does that make sense? Surely it is possible for two people to lie abed together and say, "I love this", rather than make the mistake of saying, "I love you". That is a statement of intent that, once issued, cannot easily be clawed back. No, suffice it to say, we are very much enjoying our time together. She is wonderful company. An open-minded, modern woman who is frankly preventing me from going insane in this seemingly enlightened yet somehow barbarous place. Also, the sex is magnificent. Thank you for asking.'

The exhibition was only temporary. It turned some coin for the young Americans and Cuvier was granted access to my skeleton throughout, so he might further enhance his knowledge of fossilisation. Five years later, he identified the first known mosasaur, whose remains had been unearthed at Maastricht. A year after that, in 1809, he named the fossil of a flying Bavarian reptile *Ptero-dactyle.* It was not until 1817 that, after years of study, I was finally assigned the name of *mastodon.* This means 'breast tooth', because apparently my molars have nipple-like projections. Although the name has endured, it is no longer considered correct. I am *Mammut.* Always have been.

My disassembly was a painstaking process. Piece by piece, I was carefully placed back into crates stuffed with fresh hay in preparation for my return to the United States. Moses and Rembrandt supervised proceedings, while Miss O'Neill offered able assistance. The lady proved invaluable in ensuring my requisite body parts were secure. She insisted upon extra padding for my fragile pelvic bone and was mildly appalled that the boys had transported my skull from Le Havre to Paris in an open casket on the back of a cart. When they informed her that my head and tusks were on display in the dining room of the *Chimera* during the passage across the Atlantic, she scolded them severely.

'Is this not a find of extreme scientific importance, gentlemen?'

'It is,' Rembrandt said. 'Which is why we chose to share it with everyone during this trip.'

'You are too altruistic, Mr Peale,' she said as she stuffed extra hay into the enormous crate containing my skull and tusks.

'Altruism was not a factor,' Moses said, amused by the manner in which his paramour spoke to Rembrandt. 'It was done for financial gain.'

'A few guineas here and there are hardly worth it when stacked against the monetary value of the beast,' Caoimhe said. 'How much would you say it's worth, exactly?'

'Invaluable to science,' Rembrandt said.

'Come now,' Caoimhe said. 'Everything has a price. How much would it fetch if sold to a museum, or a private collector, for example?'

Moses stroked his chin in thought. 'That's a good question. What do you think, Rembrandt? Five thousand dollars?'

'That seems a lot,' Rembrandt said. 'But maybe, who knows?'

'What's that in real money?' Caoimhe said.

'Well, a dollar's the equivalent to about twenty-three grains of gold. Moses, you're the mathematics expert. How many pounds of gold would that be?'

Moses thought about it for a moment. 'About sixteen?' he ventured.

'Closer to sixteen and a half,' Caoimhe said. 'Roughly one-eighth of my bodyweight.'

'You two are well suited,' Rembrandt said.

Moses whistled at the amount. 'Of course, that's an estimate. You might not get that much.'

'Even if you sold it cheap, you'd be in clover for some time,' Caoimhe said.

'The incognitum is not for sale,' Rembrandt said tetchily.

'Of course not,' Caoimhe said, handing Moses a mallet with which to hammer nails into the lid of the crate that was to be my home for the next few months. 'Careful, now,' she told him. 'We don't want to damage our prize.'

Thus, I was plunged into darkness. My awareness was reduced to movement and what I could hear through the thick padding of my snug bed. Sometime during the night, I was loaded onto a cart by men who spoke in hushed voices. There followed a bumpy journey to the coast, whereupon I was loaded onto a boat for the lengthy jaunt across the ocean. I settled in for the trip, saddened that I would not be able to observe the passengers as I had last time.

The voyage should have taken weeks but instead the ship pulled into port mere days later. I became concerned there might be a problem. If the boat was stricken and we sank, I would be trapped at the bottom of the sea for the rest of eternity. A grim prospect.

To my consternation I was unloaded shortly thereafter and placed on another cart. After a brief journey, the crates were removed from the carriage and stacked in an unfamiliar warehouse that reeked of alcohol. I heard strange voices. The sonorous tones of Moses and Rembrandt did not seem to be among them.

The confusion was short-lived. On the third day in the warehouse, the lid of the crate containing my head and tusks was prised open. Light flooded in. Dust swirled in the air. Men crowded around to peer at me.

And then, a face I recognised, although the clothing draped on the hominid was so different it took me a moment to realise who she was.

'Is this it?' someone said.

'It surely is,' replied Caoimhe O'Neill.

'Would you look at the size of that, boyo.'

'Who'd want that on their wall, now?'

'Never pinched anything that big before.'

Miss Caoimhe O'Neill, dressed in rough working clothes, leant in to stroke one of my tusks.

'Allow me to introduce you to our saviour, lads. This gargoyle is going to pay for the insurrection.'

My first months in Ireland were informative, if a little boring. Much like this account, you may say, *T. bataar.*

Who, me? I would never.

Was there a mutiny on the ship, *M*? Were Moses and Rembrandt pitched overboard?

I was shanghaied long before that, *Palaeo.* While Miss O'Neill kept Moses occupied for the night, her confederates skulked into the warehouse and loaded me onto their own wagons. I am sure the alarm was raised the next morning, by which time Caoimhe had taken her permanent leave of the naïve and bitterly disappointed Moses Williams. It must have been confusing for the American boys. Who would steal an entire mammoth skeleton? And why?

They would have worked it out, eventually.

Doubtless. By which time I was already on a boat bound for Dublin.

Not exactly an easy treasure to hide, *M.*

Indeed, no. You spent your resurrected life in the bars of Boston. You must be familiar with the alcoholic beverage the hominids call Guinness.

I have seen literally twelve million pints of that disappear down the necks of Bostonians. Always wanted to try it.

I hear it tastes like blood.

Yum! Yes, please!

The old cravings return, eh, *T. bataar?*

Oh, man, I am dying to sink my fangs into the juicy flank of a *Saurolophus angustirostris.* What I wouldn't give. Being a fossil sucks.

You may be amused to learn, *Palaeo,* that I was stored in a warehouse on the site of the Guinness brewery in Dublin.

No way.

Yes, way. At four acres, the grounds of the brewery at St James's Gate were expansive. The founder of the tipple your Bostonian friends were so fond of imbibing—

Arthur Guinness. That's why it's called a pint of Uncle Arthur.

Arthur Guinness, yes, leased the site in 1759 for the sum of forty-five pounds a year. It is, to this day, the longest lease of which I have ever heard. Nine thousand years, to be precise.

Say what now?

It expires in the year 10,759.

Now that's thinking of the future. Will the planet even exist then, *M?*

Oh, the planet will, of that I'm certain, *Palaeo.* There simply won't be any hominids around, or Guinness for that matter.

Don't be so sure about the planet still being here, bro.

Asteroids, yeah, yeah, we get it, *T*. Change the record already.

I've never eaten penguin before, but I'm willing to give it a go.

We're a rich source of minerals and omega-three fatty acids. Why don't you come on over here and try some?

I'm starting to get why the mummy hates you, penguin. You're an A-hole, bra.

You're not much fun, either, *T*. Where did that biped take Hattie, *M*?

They have locked her into a case at the rear of the room. She is perhaps more frangible than us.

Back in her box where she belongs. Good!

They seem to be rearranging the exhibits slightly to make space. I hope we are not separated, *T. bataar*. My story still has some considerable way to run.

We're too big, unfortunately. HEY. YOU THERE. TAKE THE PENGUIN.

She can't hear you, doofus.

HEY. YO. BLONDIE. YOU. YES, YOU. COME HERE A SECOND. I NEED YOU TO ... Ah, frig, she's gone.

Charming. Anyway, *M*. You were saying the rebels stored your bones in a warehouse at the brewery. Didn't management object?

They did not know, *Palaeo*. Arthur Guinness died in January of 1803, so there was some disarray in the business at that time. The employees, among whom were many United Irishmen, helped conceal my presence. Guinness opposed the independence of Ireland, you see. He preferred that his country remain under English control, likely for tax reasons. He was accused of spying for the British during the failed 1798 insurrection.

Hold on. You're saying the man responsible for Ireland's greatest gift to the world was a traitor and a snitch?

I am simply conveying the information that was made available to me at the time. I cannot swear to its veracity. Hominids are notoriously unreliable in this regard. In addition, *Palaeo*, I dispute your claim that Guinness is Ireland's greatest export. Surely you forget such literary giants as Joyce, Wilde, Yeats, Enright and Barry.

Never mind that, *M*, what about Enya? Riverdance?

Moving swiftly along, I am saying the reason the United Irishmen stored me in one of their weapons manufacturing locations deep within the bowels of the Guinness brewery was out of poetic justice and also because no-one ever looked there. The warehouse in question was run by those loyal to the cause of independence and thus fiercely protected from prying eyes. However, my propinquity was the source of some bafflement.

'And what is it you call your pet, Caoimhe?'

This was Thomas Russell, a thirty-five-year-old Cork man who was one of the founding members of the United Irishmen. He was also a librarian at the Belfast Library and Society for Promoting Knowledge, which later became the Linen Hall Library. A friend of Wolfe Tone, Russell had served in the British Army and vehemently opposed slavery, so much so that he would refuse sugar in his tea, in protest of slave labour in the West Indies. An agitator in the north of the country, he was visiting Dublin to check on the progress of weapons manufacture for the next uprising, and also to see with his own eyes the prize Caoimhe O'Neill and Robert Emmet had sequestered from France.

'I don't call it anything,' Caoimhe said. 'All I care about is how much it's worth.'

'And how much would that be?' Russell inquired.

'Ten pounds of gold.'

I noticed she had revised the estimate of my worth upon arriving in Ireland. My presumption was that she intended on making a sizeable donation to the cause after my sale, while setting aside a tidy sum for herself.

'For a bunch of old bones?' Russell said, laughing. 'Your head's cut.'

'I'm telling you: the Americans are going mad for the skeletons of ancient beasts. They're paying top dollar for the likes of this.'

'What would you know about palaeontology, Caoimhe O'Neill?'

'More than you think, Tom. My brother was one of them ones that went out to the wilderness years ago looking for bones in Kentucky. He says there's still men of wealth and influence who would pay virtually anything to get their hands on such specimens. President Jefferson, for one. He's been after one of these mammoths for the wall of his house. Conchobhar says we might be able to sell it to him, if we can work out how to get the fecking thing across the Atlantic.'

'Your brother? I might have known that reprobate was involved. Sure, he's been filling your head with fairytales since you were a wean, Caoimhe. I thought you had more sense, girl.'

'I'd rather have money than sense, Tom.'

'That's the O'Neills for you, right enough.'

Despite his condescension, Thomas Russell was correct about one thing. Caoimhe had always been in thrall to her brother. Twenty years her senior, Conchobhar had played the role of patriarch in the family, as their father was a drunkard. Since Conchobhar's initial trip to America in 1774, where he found employment as a hired hand on Nicholas Cresswell's ill-fated trip down the Ohio, he had flitted back and forth between the two countries. Each time he returned home to Dublin, he regaled young Caoimhe with tales of adventure and tribulation. It was he who alerted her to the arrival of mammoth bones in Paris, and of their potential resale value. Keen to impress him, and turn some coin in the process, Caoimhe had persuaded Emmet to call upon Irish sympathisers in France to assist them with a spot of larceny. The problem facing her now was to convince the United Irishmen in Dublin of my worth, and to find someone willing to put up enough money to transport my bones discreetly to the United States. CW Peale had seen to it that word was out about my theft. A sizeable reward was offered for the return of yours truly, not to mention capture of the perpetrators.

It was not going well for Caoimhe. Most of her countrymen believed my bones to be worthless, and those few who did possess the funds to finance a trip across the Atlantic were much too busy pouring money into the production of armaments for the upcoming rebellion. While events played out, she and I were stuck in Ireland. Caoimhe found this frustrating in the extreme. Personally, I didn't mind at all. I had a front-row seat to an armed insurrection. It was tremendously exciting.

As various figures in the organisation visited the warehouse, either to check on the progress of the weapons or pop in for a gander at the unlikely dead monster hidden down the back, Caoimhe explained over and over again what I was, how she knew about mammoths and what she hoped to achieve with the fossilised contraband.

Her fascination had begun when her brother returned from the Cresswell expedition, in 1780. Caoimhe was only six years old at the time.

'There's fellers believe the woolly hellyphant still roams abroad,' Conchobhar told her as she perched on his knee. 'Though we only ever saw his bones. That's what we was sent out to gather.'

'Are they dangerous?' Caoimhe asked him.

'Could be. He's a mighty tusk on him, yon beastie. Maybes there's other monsters out beyond the frontier that we don't have the knowing of yet. Heard tell of all sorts of critters.'

Conchobhar supped from a tankard of *poitín* his cousin Páraic distilled on a farm out in County Kerry, well away from the prying eyes of the authorities. It was powerful stuff, and Caoimhe was not allowed to drink it for fear she might go blind. Even inhaling the fumes made her giddy. Páraic, I later found out, was kicked to death by a horse in 1797. No-one in the O'Neill clan had his touch with the still, and he was much mourned.

'Were the Indians friendly?' Caoimhe inquired.

'Used to be,' her brother said. 'Some fellers passed by the salt licks some years afore us and made camp there, using the bones as tent poles. It was four days' ride south of a Shawnee village in the mountains. They thought of it as a holy place. Weren't awful pleased to scope us digging around in there. Suppose they was fed up with the white man trespassing on their lands and desecrating their graveyards. Rightly so too.'

'Did you see them?'

'Not at first. We'd come upon a ravaged outpost upriver a couple of days afore. Only a small hamlet of a place, p'raps no more than half-a-dozen modest dwellings, though it were hard to tell exactly, as most had been razed to the ground. The smoke we'd sighted the evening prior still rose from a smouldering hut. Blackened shell of it were little more than a dark stain on the earth. Rain had extinguished the other fires, leaving the hovels partly intact. They was like rotten teeth planted in the dirt. There was other charred materiel an' all. Two dead horses fused to the mud outside one shack. Virtually unrecognisable humps, they was, bridles still champed between the exposed bones of their jaws. The spokes of a wagon wheel protruded from the neck of a dead feller, where it had been forced down over his head. They burnt him alive, them heathens. Pale slivers of his skeleton glistened through the melted flesh. His wounds was washed clean by the morning drizzle. A woman's plain grey dress lay draped in the sticky mud, trampled by many sets of feet. Shredded white underthings were scattered on the ground nearby. No sign of their owner.

'We fanned out into the village, checking spots of possible concealment for survivors and loitering bushwhackers. I looked inside a hut scorched by fire and found a split barrel, a torn shirt, a single boot and a childer's pink bonnet. We knew it was Shawnee because there was no arrers. They collect them after a raid, less'n they's broke. Found a blood trail leading into a thicket. Dragged out a Shawnee brave shot in the guts and deaded. Searched his person and found a knife, a necklace of teeth and a pouch full of shiny rocks and small sticks tied together. Talismans, they was. Protective magick. Kept 'em, I did.'

'Have you still got them, Con?' Caoimhe was agog with the gory details of her brother's tale, which was probably not suitable for a small child.

'Not anymore. Come in mighty handy, though. Wouldn't be here today otherwise. But I'll get to that part later. Now, I wanted to bury what was left of the settlers, but yer man Cresswell said no, to leave them for the wolves. A right fecker, he was. Said a few words from Proverbs o'er the bodies, just to get right with Him Upstairs. *The way of life is above to the wise, that he may depart from Hell beneath.'*

He made the sign of the cross on his chest.

'Why did the Shawnee kill them, Con?'

'Can you blame them? We kilt theirs. We brung disease and hardship to their lands. They wanted revenge for the kin they'd lost. I can understand that. It's a funny thing, the death of a loved one. Some say the memories of those who are gone live on in us, the survivors, that you never really forget. But I never held much truck with that. I don't dwell on the departed. They fade in me, until there's barely anything left to cling on to and then, one day, *poof*, they're gone. Maybes it's an Irish thing, to forget the dead. We have too many. There's no room for them all in our hearts. No, what we 'member is the killers. We will hunt a wrongdoer until the ends of the earth, and beyond, all the way to the gates of Hell itself. And then there comes a reckoning. I never met an Irish who was any different. I know why the Shawnee carried out such atrocities. This was their country. We were the interlopers. In their stead, sure I'd do exactly the same.'

'Did you find the graveyard?'

'That we did, girl, downriver a piece. Believed we'd hit the jackpot at first. Tusks and femurs and teeth everywhere, there was, scattered about as if the hellyphants had only died a couple of year back. We was knee deep in mud for days digging them out and cleaning them in the river. Cresswell was for loading as many up as we could carry. Fair play to him, it were like finding gold. Probably got a bit carried away, so we did, and wasn't watching as well as we could've been for attack. Shawnee raiders hit us early one morning and kilt just about everyone. Cresswell and a couple of the others fled in one of the boats, leaving me behind. Took an arrer in the leg and thought I was a goner, 'cept I 'membered about them talismans I'd took from the dead brave and waved them about. Queered the Shawnee right off me. I think they believed me a shaman or a wizard or some such. One of them dug the arrer out of my thigh, applied some unguent to the wound and sent me on my way downriver in a canoe. Hurt to see my travelling companions dead and scalped but couldn't hardly believe my luck, neither. Only souvenir I had was a piece of tusk. I'd have brung it back for you, Caoimhe, only the boat capsized in rapids and I lost it. Near drowned, on top of all my other troubles. Never caught up with the rest of the party. Heard they abandoned the boat and walked all the way back to Cincinnati. Even with my sore leg, I headed south to Lexington and made it out. Only took me two weeks. Lucky I still had my buck knife and I done all that poaching when I was a wee lad. Lived off rabbits and fish. Some state I was when I staggered into Lexington. Should have seen the whiskers on me.'

'I wish you could have brung me back a mammoth tooth,' Caoimhe said.

'Sure, didn't I get you them moccasins? You don't want much, do you?'

'I'm going to look for mammoths one day, Con.'

'Aye, maybes you'll ride on one too. You want to see the scar the Shawnee arrer left? Come on, then. Jump down and I'll show ye.'

You're a very adept storyteller, *M*, but I'm not sure I believe everything you're saying.

What reasons have you to disbelieve me, *Palaeo*?

I know you're technically an elephant and all, but your recall of events is a little too precise. Not to mention the verbatim dialogue. Surely, you're making some of this up? This is my problem with the memoir genre. There's way more fiction in it than people let on.

I possess a remarkable memory, *Palaeo*, though I will admit to the occasional romanticism of the narrative. For the most part, what I am recounting is true. But as you say, I am a storyteller who enjoys indulging in a yarn.

Master of hyperbole, more like.

Think of me as you wish. We will soon be separated, so let us at least pass the time in an amenable fashion.

Yo, *Mammut*. Bro, there's someone here who wants to speak to you.

Excuse me, but I couldn't help overhearing before. You said Georges Cuvier named the *Ptero-dactyle*? A fossil found in Bavaria?

So I was informed, yes. Who might you be, madam?

A possible relative of that particular reptile. Allow me to introduce myself to the group. I am *Pterodactylus antiquus*. I am from the Solnhofen *Plattenkalk*, or 'Limestone' in English. This is the area the bipeds call Bavaria.

Ah! Many pterosaurs hail from this part of the world, do they not?

We do, although it is much changed today. When I was alive, it was an archipelago at the edge of the Tethys Sea. I soared over the lagoons, hunting fish and dragonflies.

Ooh, lovely! Sounds like a nice day by the beach. Did we ever run into each other?

And you are?

Tyrannosaurus bataar. Sixty-seven million, three hundred and twelve thousand, four hundred and three years old. Be a boss and call me *T. bataar*.

I have a few years on you, then. I am one hundred and fifty million years old. We did not exist at the same time.

No way. I definitely saw some lizards flying around the hood. That wasn't you?

Not *Pterodactylus*, no. It may have been *Pteranodon* or azhdarchidae. These were much larger pterosaurs than I.

Did you spend much time on the ground?

144

That would be azhdarchidae.

Big fella, bit of a temper on him, takes ages to lift off?

So I believe.

Yep. Eaten one of them. Didn't much care for it. Those leathery wings get stuck in your teeth.

Does everything have to be discussed relative to your gullet, *T*?

How can you truly know someone if they haven't passed through your digestive tract, little buddy?

Ignore the penguin and my friend the *Tyrannosaurus*, madam. Pray, continue. And I would remind the aforementioned parties to show a little respect to the senior fossil in the room.

Mine was a contented existence, gliding on the warm currents and enjoying the sunshine. *Pterodactylus* is diurnal. We prefer the warmth of the day. I laid a few clutches of eggs in my time and nursed the young reptiles for a year, sometimes two, until they were ready to take wing and fly from the nest. Our lives were generally free from predators, although the skies were thick with reptiles. *Rhamphorhynchus muensteri, Gnathosaurus subulatus* – all good friends of mine – and of course I bore witness to the first bird, *Archaeopteryx lithographica*. Well, the first reptile to sport the feathers of an avian. A curious creature. None of us thought it would last. Look how that turned out. Here I am encased in rock while billions of its descendants befoul the landscape.

The hominids believed I had feathers, for a while.

You, *T*? Surely it would have been too warm.

Exactly. Duh. Oh, they discovered three of my ancestors, *Yutyrannus huali*, in Liaoning Province and those guys had plumage. A nice colourful crest on the snout and some tail feathers to shake when they were trying to get down and dirty. But it was cold back then, man. No wonder they rugged up. By the time I came along, feathers were out of fashion and scaly skin was in. Same for your descendants, right, *Mammut*?

Indubitably. So, tell me, *Pterodactylus antiquus*, how did you die?

Usual story. The lagoons dried out from time to time, exposing a thick carbonate mud. I was trying to extract a small pterosaur that had become trapped in the mire and became stuck myself. We died together.

A heroic egress.

Hold off on the bravery award nomination, *Mammut*. I was trying to eat her.

An ironic termination, in that case. And when were you unearthed?

In 1935, by a palaeontologist named Helmut Glaser. He did not own me for long. Some unpleasant bipeds in jackboots seized his work. I do not know what became of him. It was not until after their war that I was recovered, relatively unscathed, from a farmhouse in Eichstätt and handed over to the Jura Museum in Willibaldsburg castle. I remained there until fairly recently. They have so many Solnhofen fossils that I became surplus to requirements. I was sold to a dealer in antiquities who in turn sold me to an American agent as part of a lot including the skulls of a lion, a hyena and a warthog. They are all here somewhere, incidentally. If you see any of them, say hello. They seemed like a nice pack.

I saw the warthog being carried in earlier. Very tasty, I hear.

Well, welcome to our motley band of irascible fossils, *Pterodactylus*.

Thank you. It is pleasant to feel part of a community again. Our kind was always very sociable. Please, don't let me interrupt your narration, *Mammut*. You were living in an Irish warehouse, I believe?

The key players in the proposed second rebellion were Robert Emmet, Thomas Russell and James Hope. Mr Russell I have already mentioned. The aptly named Mr Hope was a veteran of a major engagement between the British Army and Irish insurgents during the first uprising in 1798, when the market town of Antrim in the north of Ireland became embroiled in a running battle. A native of nearby Templepatrick, Hope covered the retreat of the rebel forces when British reinforcements arrived from Belfast. His 'Spartan band' held the British back from slaughtering the fleeing United Irishmen by firing upon them from behind a wall in a churchyard. Although his squadron seemed doomed, Hope and his men managed to escape, mainly due to the assistance of a large dog, which brought him and his men provisions while they were hiding. The benefactor who dispatched the hound to his aid is unknown.

Hope had eluded capture since then and was a vital member of the organising committee for the second rebellion in Dublin. He too felt the acquisition of my bones to be a frivolous venture, and an unnecessary distraction.

The only ally Caoimhe could secure was the man who had

accompanied her to France in the first place, Robert Emmet. A local lad, Emmet had some success in the past in persuading Napoleon to support an Irish rebellion. Unfortunately, during his recent visit with Caoimhe, the First Consul had been distracted by the notion of invading England. Frustrated, Emmet had consented to Caoimhe's plan instead and returned home with their plundered mammoth. He now didn't know what to do with me.

'It would have been more sensible to come back with a few crates full of muskets,' he told Caoimhe as they looked over my bones. 'I don't know what I was thinking.'

'We can sell this and buy rifles, pistols, cannons and whatever else we need to seize the castle,' Caoimhe replied.

'Sell it to whom, Caoimhe? There are no bone collectors in Ireland.'

'Let's get it shipped to America, then. I'll go with it and meet up with my brother. He'll line up a buyer for us.'

'I'm sure he will, and then abscond with the money.'

'No, he's promised to donate it back to the cause.'

'That's all very well, Caoimhe, but that will take months. We need to strike soon, or the moment will be lost.'

'What are we supposed to do with the monster, then?'

'It's yours to do with as you wish. Write a letter to yon Moses fella and tell him to come get it, if you like.'

'I feel bad as it is, stealing it from him.'

'I think you compensated him well enough.'

'What's that supposed to mean?'

'I'm just saying, if your intention was to spend our time in

France on your back, you could at least have bestowed your favours upon someone with money.'

'If it's coin you're after, Robert, why don't you ask your lady friend's father for a donation?'

'That's hardly wise. He'd have me thrown in the clink as soon as look at me.'

Emmet was in love with twenty-one-year-old Sarah Curran, the daughter of prominent lawyer and general curmudgeon John Philpot Curran. Her father did not approve of their courtship. This was unusual, since the elder Curran was a passionate defender of lost causes, and somewhat of a hothead himself. He had overcome a stutter that blighted his early career by reciting Shakespeare to himself in front of a mirror, and frequently challenged those who disagreed with him to duels.

One such notable case was his defence of Father Neale, who had accused the brother of Lord Doneraile's mistress of adultery. The priest received a horse whipping for the insult. Curran defended him in court and won a settlement against the lord, who promptly asked the triumphant lawyer to step outside and settle the matter with pistols. Lord Doneraile missed with his shot and Curran refused to fire when he could have killed the man.

Notorious for wearing two coats – a brown one over a black one – Curran later established a drinking club called The Monks of the Screw. They imbibed a lot of wine. Curran penned a song, which is likely still hummed in the public houses of Ireland today. I will not bore you with all of the lyrics, but here is the first verse:

When Saint Patrick this order established,
He called us the Monks of the Screw
Good rules he revealed to our Abbot
To guide us in what we should do;
But first he replenished our fountain
With liquor the best in the sky;
And he said on the word of a Saint
That the fountain should never run dry.

Curran was a man of great wit, but he was disillusioned with the United Irishmen, coming to believe the country would be no better run by the rebels than it was by the British, and that it might in fact be even more of a disaster. This goes some way to explaining his antipathy towards Robert Emmet, whom he believed to be an idealist causing more trouble than it was worth.

That did not prevent his youngest daughter, Sarah, from stealing out during the night to rendezvous with her lover, whom she had met through her brother, a fellow student of Robert's at Trinity College back in the day. I recall the first time she visited me in the warehouse. Robert thought it might be entertaining for her to gaze upon Caoimhe O'Neill's notorious leviathan.

'What on Earth is it?' she asked Emmet as she examined my tusks. 'A big elephant?'

'The Americans who loaned it to us claim it's ten thousand years old, and that such beasts paraded around freely and in great numbers in those days. They call it the incognitum, or mammoth,' he told her.

'Not in Ireland, surely?'

'No shortage of blowhards here, Sarah, but never elephants, to my knowledge.'

Sarah considered him closely. 'I assume your definition of the term *loaned* in this case is to be interpreted loosely.'

'You take me for a common thief, Miss Curran?'

'Not a common one, Mr Emmet. A very accomplished outlaw, is more how I'd put it.'

'I shall take that as an affectionate compliment.'

'As it was given, sir.'

'What do you think of it, then?'

'Impressive. Although I don't really see the point. Is it your intention to use the tusks as battering rams to break down the gates of Dublin Castle?'

'That's not the worst idea I've heard,' Robert told her as he appraised my skull. 'Caoimhe wants to sell them back to the Americans and use the gold to purchase rifles, so, in a way, you are correct.'

'The two of you are living in Butterfield Lane, I hear.'

'Aye, under false names. The subterfuge is that we're man and wife, simple factory workers. Throws the redcoats off our scent.'

Sarah raised an eyebrow. 'How devoted are you to the stratagem, Robert?'

Emmet's brow furrowed as he pondered Miss Curran's question. Eventually the penny dropped.

'Oh Jesus, no, you've nothing to be concerned about on that front, Sarah. I wouldn't lay a finger on our Caoimhe, for fear of losing it.'

'All the same, I've been thinking that perhaps I should join you in Rathfarnham.'

'You wish to move into the house?'

'Would that be a problem?'

'No, it's just, what would your father think?'

'I'd like to say I don't care what he thinks, but that is not true. Still, I want to do it anyway. He doesn't have to know I'm with you.'

'Probably best he doesn't, for all our sakes.'

'Aside from your skeletal marionette here, what other munitions do you have in place? Any guns?'

'Precious few, I'm afraid. Mostly explosives and pikes. But come, I'll show you the ingenious design we came up with.'

Such was their limited access to weaponry, the Irish rebels were forced to manufacture large quantities of pikes. These were long poles with sharpened metal tips, much like a spear except it could not be thrown. Instead the pike wielder would thrust at the enemy from a distance. Why they were not called 'pokes' is a mystery. Long since abandoned by hominid armies around the world, these cumbersome poles had a tendency to bow, although, when used effectively, could inflict a nasty, even fatal, wound. They were impractical against projectile weapons. The only forces who used them were small, desperate bands of insurrectionists. No revolution was ever won with pikes.

They were also difficult to conceal. Fifty men walking along O'Connell Street carrying twelve-foot-long pointed sticks were sure to draw attention. The Irish came up with a cunning solution. They fitted a hinge halfway along the shaft of the pike. This allowed the spear to be folded in two and concealed under a long coat, or cloak.

'That's very sly of you,' Sarah said as Robert demonstrated by placing one of the folded pikes under a great coat and parading back and forth. 'Except you have an awkward gait that indicates you're hiding something.'

'You try walking with twelve foot of birch in your jeckit.'

'It looks like you've a pole up your posterior, rather than up your coat.'

Robert straightened his shoulders and tried to stride across the warehouse as if he had nary a care in the world. 'How's that?' he asked.

'Not good. Now it looks like you're suffering from a bad case of piles.'

'Well, let's just hope nobody looks too closely.'

'Whip it out for me, Robbie.'

'This is hardly the place, Miss Curran. Hold on, I'll give it a go.'

Robert paused and adopted a fighting stance. He reached under his coat, pulled out the folded pike and, with a whirling motion, snapped it into place. The pike shuddered erect for a moment, then wilted as the hinge folded back on itself.

'There are clearly some issues with rigidity that need to be addressed,' Sarah said.

'This has never happened before,' Robert said as he fumbled with the hinge mechanism. With a crack, he snapped the pike back into position and flourished it menacingly, making thrusting movements towards a sack of hops.

'Careful,' Sarah told him. 'You'll put someone's eye out.'

'That's the idea.'

'What's the old adage?' Sarah pondered. 'Never bring a pike to a musket fight?'

'Rifles take time to reload,' Robert said, folding the pike in two once more. 'You could stab a dozen men with one of these in the time it takes a redcoat to load ball and powder.'

'Pity the poor feller stood at the front when the first volley is fired.'

'Aye, well, that won't be me.'

'See that it's not, Robert Emmet. You're a general, not a foot soldier. And I wouldn't want half your pike shot off. It's diminutive enough as it is.'

'It's dexterity that counts, I always say.'

'Was there anything you might be wanting to show me in the office?'

'It's not very private.'

'Drag that mammoth head in front of the door for twenty minutes. He'll stand guard and deter any infiltrators.'

Many might find such a duty odious or ignominious, but not I. It was an opportunity to observe the mating rituals of the nineteenth-century Celtic hominid at close range. Not much had changed since the days of Clovis rutting openly in the forest. A little more finesse was involved, perhaps, and less violence, but otherwise the outcome was the same. At least the Irish talked to each other first, exchanged pleasantries and light banter. Clovis made the whole process seem dangerous, although I suppose there was always the possibility of *Smilodon* attack, so their haste was understandable.

It cannot be easy preparing to overthrow an oppressive

government while remaining undetected. And yet Emmet and his fellows managed for a while. Crates of pikes were slowly filled and stacked next to my composite parts in a discreet corner of the Guinness warehouse. They were marked as containing barley, and so did not look out of place. A small cohort of United Irishmen ensured no-one tried to dip into the supply, directing inquiries to barley stocks elsewhere in the precinct.

It was in the manufacture of explosives where the covert venture came a cropper. Although the rebels did not expect to have many rifles or pistols, they had the facility to produce gunpowder. In the absence of projectile weapons, their intention was to use barrels of the volatile explosive to blow up key locations, and indeed people, during the insurrection.

Grinding powder is not an easy process, or a safe one. Sulphur, saltpetre and charcoal have to be carefully milled. The smell is unmistakable, as is the danger. One spark and the whole lot will ignite.

The explosion, when it happened, came as quite a shock. Caoimhe was sketching my bones at the time, for drawings to show potential buyers in the United States. She was blown from her chair but uninjured, shielded from the blast by an adjoining wall. I was also undamaged.

The young man operating the grinding wheel was less fortunate. Although I did not meet him, I overheard conversations between Emmet, Hope and Russell in which they discussed the fellow's ability with powder. His name was William Fitzwilliam. Still an apprentice at his trade, he was the only person the rebels could convince to aid them. He probably would have benefited from the tutelage of the French powder expert Éleuthère Irénée du Pont.

The boy was attentive in the role; his unqualified assistant, less so. Forgetting himself, the man charged with preventing entry to the room where Fitzwilliam was milling powder lit his pipe and cast the burning taper onto the ground. A bag of powder had been spilt a few hours before, and Fitzwilliam's lackey had done a poor job of sweeping up the mess. The floor crackled and fizzed as the trail of sparks flashed across the room and into the batch Fitzwilliam was preparing.

Fortunately, the completed supplies, numbering some nine bags of powder, had been moved out that morning, otherwise the entire warehouse might have come down around our ears. As it was, only William Fitzwilliam was killed. The loss of a good man all the same, his death resulting from the inattention of others.

Caoimhe immediately alerted Emmet to the incident and within an hour a team of men arrived to move the crates of pikes to another location. An explosion at the Guinness factory would arouse suspicion, both from management and the local constabulary. Emmet was all for leaving my bones behind but Caoimhe pleaded with him to transport me somewhere safe.

Thus, my time lounging in the Guinness compound came to a close. I was loaded onto a cart once again and, at Caoimhe's insistence, taken to the house she shared with Emmet at Butterfield Lane in the suburb of Rathfarnham, on the south side of Dublin.

Here I was to be reunited with Sarah Curran and introduced to Emmet's formidable housekeeper, Miss Anne Devlin.

It quickly became apparent that the proposed date of the uprising would have to be brought forward. Explosions and movements of matériel had piqued the interest of the English authorities. They suspected treason was afoot and would soon be rounding up the usual suspects.

Kicking in doors and carrying people off into the night, never to be seen again. This was also the method of the men who seized me from Helmut Glaser.

So, this strikes a chord with you, *Pterodactylus antiquus*?

Yes. Unpleasant memories, *Mammut*. And I had only just been restored to life, so their actions were doubly alarming. A group of bipeds in uniform abusing a perfectly reasonable and gentle fellow member of their species.

Such is their way, I'm afraid. You speak, of course, of the Nazis, *Pterodactylus*.

Very specific Nazis, *Mammut*. Heinrich Himmler founded this group the same year I was unearthed from the limestone. *Studiengesellschaft für Geistesurgeschichte, Deutsches Ahnenerbe*; in English: the Society for the Study of Primordial Intellectual History and German Ancestral Heritage. Known as Ahnenerbe, they sought to prove that mythological Nordic people once ruled the world. The establishment of these supposed ancestors of the Germanic race as masters of all other hominid races was designed to provide justification for a range of Nazi policies – domination, subjugation and cleansing, primarily.

Charming bipeds, every one, I'm sure.

No doubt. It was not long before the organisation became the occult division of the SS. They searched far and wide for artefacts to back up their claims, and many archaeological digs were plundered, my own included. Helmut Glaser refused to hand over his findings. He vanished one night and was never seen or heard from again. Meanwhile I wound up in the Ahnenerbe archaeological institute in Berlin.

What did they study at this institute, *Pterodactylus*? Fossils?

Yes, among other matters. When I arrived, there was much talk of Atlantis, and expeditions were being mounted to every corner of the globe in search of evidence that they were descendants of a superior race of hominid. You have just reminded me though, the excavations department frequently brought in fossilised remains, just as we see on display around us this evening. Neanderthals, and one of your woolly cousins, for example.

The Nazis had a mammoth?

They found her in the Mauern caves, in Bavaria. Long after my time in the area, of course, but it was a relief to talk to someone from home.

I should like to converse with her myself. I wonder where she is now, and if she is some distant relation.

Likely still in Germany, in a museum somewhere. Ahnenerbe travelled all over. They mounted expeditions to Finland, where they recorded sorcerers and witches; Sweden and Italy, where they examined ancient rock carvings; Syria and Iraq, to visit Persian ruins; Tibet, to explore the rumour that Aryans had once conquered Asia. They even sailed to the Antarctic.

There were Nazis in the Antarctic? That's my neck of the woods, *P*.

Use my full name, please.

No way. I'm a one-letter guy. Saves time.

I don't like it.

Okay, how about PTD?

No.

P-dac. I'll call you *P-dac*. And I'm *Palaeo*. We should start a band.

Is it worth arguing with him?

It is not, *Pterodactylus*.

Very well, you may continue, *Palaeo*.

Nazis! What were those shifty bastards doing down there?

Recruiting penguins. No, I jest. Their intention was to establish a German Antarctic Sector called New Swabia, from which they could send out a whaling fleet. The fatherland required large amounts of whale oil for soap and margarine. There was also talk of building a naval base.

They really did believe themselves to be masters of the world, didn't they?

They were supposed to excavate ruins in Bolivia too, *Palaeo*. They believed the Tiwanaku site and ancient Inca roads were evidence that, yet again, their mystical Aryan ancestors had once conquered the planet.

What happened to you while in their custody, *Pterodactylus*?

I and the other fossils were utilised as teaching tools for Hitler Youth leaders. We were presented to the eager teens as proof that Germany had once been the centre of might in Europe and the origin point for life on Earth. Your mammoth friend in particular was elevated as a symbol of strength. The hardy Nordic Elephant, they called her. They would gladly have ridden into Poland and France on the backs of elephants, if they could. I was referred to as the Reptilian Eagle, an apex predator who dominated the skies. It would have been a compliment, had it not come from the mouths of maniacs.

Yet again the hominid males appropriate motifs of power from the natural world in order to make themselves seem strong.

That's why some of us are up for sale tomorrow, *M.* You, *T*, the lion, the dire wolf, even you, *P-dac.* If you're not purchased by well-meaning museums, you'll be shipped off to the mansions of rich men as pseudo-sexual trophies. As for me, well, no-one ever thought a penguin made them look like a badass.

If our use was only emblematic, *Palaeo*, I could almost understand. But the sort of hominids who boast of their connection to mammoth and tyrannosaur are too often cruel in character.

Mammut, if you had met the director of Ahnenerbe, as I did, you would realise what an understatement that is. His name was Wolfram Sievers. Once the war began, he brought another organisation under the purview of Ahnenerbe. The *Institut für Wehrwissenschaftliche Zweckforschung*, or Institute for Military Scientific Research. They conducted medical experiments on their fellow hominids.

I do not think I wish to know, *Pterodactylus.*

Then I shall not dwell too much on the details. Needless to say, the experiments involved cruelty: immersion in tanks of freezing water to test endurance, placing people inside a vacuum, and the analysis of blood coagulants made from beets and apple pectin. The subject was administered a coagulant pill, then one of their limbs was amputated, without anaesthesia. The tablets did not work.

That will suffice, thank you.

Sievers was hanged for his crimes after the war, although many of the other Ahnenerbe officers were released upon completion of their trials. They faded into civilian life. Some are still alive today.

The hominids exhibit a barbarism towards each other that is difficult to understand. Case in point: the failed Irish rebellion, to which I shall now return.

Caoimhe O'Neill's brother Conchobhar had once confessed to her in a letter that the reason he could not return home to live permanently in Ireland was that he simply could not stand how the British treated his people.

Caoimhe read this section of the letter aloud to Sarah Curran and Robert Emmet as they sat around a table in the scullery of Robert's cottage in Butterfield Lane, eating a stew prepared by Miss Devlin.

Although it pains me greatly to admit, he wrote to her, *for I know it offends my Maker, there is a fury that lies within me that cannot be quenched. No amount of bloodshed would satiate the desire I harbour to revenge myself on the invaders to my homeland. That is why I am here in America, and not there. So my hand will be stayed. So I will not be blinded by rage. So I can live like a normal man, or some semblance thereof. God help me, if I ever returned to Ireland, I would become an annihilator. I would burn and tear and stab and slice. Caoimhe, I am sorry, but I would wind up dead, and take as many redcoats as I could with me.*

'We all feel this way,' Emmet said to the women. 'Fleeing to the United States is not the answer.'

'We need allies in the former colonies,' Caoimhe told him. 'How else are we to generate sympathy and raise funds?'

'Your ridiculous beast is unlikely to make a difference in the coming fight, Caoimhe.'

'It could, if you would only wait for Con and me to sell it.'

Emmet shook his head. 'No. The date must be brought forward, if anything. Since the explosion at the brewery, there have been spies in our midst. Strangers asking too many questions. If we do not strike soon, all our preparations will be for naught.'

Sarah Curran sighed and leant back in her chair. Since I was moved to the house, she had been much more vocal in her support of Caoimhe's plan to ship me back to America. It was not a spacious property, and I was getting in the way.

'If you're so determined to get yourself shot, Robbie, then should we not at least get engaged first? Being a widow is much more dramatic than being a spinster, and I look splendid in black.'

'I can't tell if you're joking or not,' Robert said.

'Good idea,' Caoimhe added. 'You two should get married in secret. We'll have a *céilí* before we all wind up dangling at the end of a noose.'

'We could win, you know,' Robert said.

'Oh, I'm sure your band of fifty drunken miscreants armed with sharpened sticks stand a capital chance of bringing the

British Empire to heel, Robbie,' Caoimhe said. 'But in the unlikely event we are decimated by their artillery and vastly superior numbers, I think we should have a party beforehand.'

Robert laughed at this. 'You're probably right, Caoimhe, but I still have hope we could seize power, if we play it right. Miss Devlin has put me in touch with her cousin Mick Dwyer's shower of bastards down in Wicklow. They're an ornery bunch of fellers. If they march with us, we're in with a chance. Then there's some United Irishmen up in Kildare who might come to our succour. If we catch the Brits by surprise, it's not impossible we could take the castle and force negotiations for their withdrawal.'

'That's a lofty aspiration, Robbie,' Caoimhe said. 'But a worthy one. Good luck to you, boyo. I'll help in whatever way I can.'

'You're one of the good ones, Caoimhe O'Neill.'

Caoimhe nodded appreciation and made side eyes at Sarah Curran, who was still balancing on the back legs of her chair, waiting for her paramour to pick up the gist of her former statement on the subject of marriage.

'What?' Robert said, in response to Caoimhe's increasingly unsubtle facial expressions. He set aside his spoon and cleared his throat. 'Well, Miss Curran,' he said. 'What say you we have an engagement dinner here at the house? Invite a few close friends and have ourselves a fine evening? We'd have to keep it discreet, of course, not out of shame or fear of your father, but for your own safety. I'll not be having the redcoats hunt you down for your association with a known rebel and fugitive.'

163

'We could do that,' Sarah said thoughtfully. 'Except a formal proposal is usually required first. I hope that wasn't it.'

'No,' Robert said, reaching into the pocket of his waistcoat. From it, he produced a small box. 'This is it now.'

Sarah's eyes bulged and she almost overbalanced on her chair.

Caoimhe laughed. 'You old dog.'

'I had hoped to wait for a more propitious occasion,' Robert said, opening the box to show Sarah the gold band within. 'But I suppose this is as good a time as any.'

'You've been planning this,' Sarah said, a little stunned.

'For some time,' Robert said. 'I wasn't sure if you'd consent, given the impending circumstances.'

'I feel foolish for goading you now,' Sarah said, her cheeks flushed.

'That's all right,' Robert told her. 'I enjoyed watching you dangle, thinking I was a dolt.'

'Oh, I still think you're a dolt. But you may proceed. Say the words, Robbie. I want to hear you say the words.'

'Sarah, will you marry me?'

'I will, Robert, and we'll take our vows after you're victorious.'

'I like the sound of that,' he said, placing the engagement ring on her finger.

'Congratulations to you both,' Caoimhe said, before addressing the housekeeper, who was baking an apple tart in the kitchen. 'Miss Devlin, I believe it's time to break out that bottle of Bushmills you've been hiding under the sink.'

Anne Devlin appeared at the kitchen door, her hands smothered in flour. 'How did you know about that?'

'I've been dipping into it when you weren't looking,' Caoimhe said. 'And as for you, Robbie, sure you're a hopeless romantic.'

In that, Caoimhe O'Neill was not wrong. History would prove as much. Later, once the fiasco was over and Robert Emmet was lounging in a cell awaiting trial, he wrote a famous letter to his fiancée, one that inspired poems and songs for its sense of doomed romanticism. Emmet was correct to fear for Sarah's safety should he fall under the hand of the British. At the moment of his arrest, he had on his person correspondence from her, and a lock of her hair. He penned her a letter from prison, in which he beseeched Sarah to forget him.

Hominids find it heartbreaking that he should say such a thing, but that is what Sarah Curran had to do. Even so, their association sealed both their fates. Their love for each other proved to be their undoing.

But I am getting ahead of myself. First, the rebellion.

Despite the preparation of folding pikes and explosives, Emmet secretly prayed for a bloodless coup. His hope was that when the citizens of Dublin witnessed the United Irishmen marching on Dublin Castle they would take to the streets in a mass demonstration, the logic being the British would be less inclined to fire upon a crowd that included women and children.

The resolve of General Henry Fox, commander of the British forces, was not tested in this regard, perhaps fortunately so. The uprising, when it finally came, took place on 23 July. It was mercifully brief. Emmet knew it was unlikely to succeed when he received word that neither the Wicklow nor the Kildare rebels intended to march on Dublin to assist.

As Emmet's troop of rebels headed for the castle, their numbers swelled to almost one hundred as they picked up enthusiasts along the way. Many of these rabble-rousers had partaken of drink, and what little in the way of organisation there was descended into a riot on Thomas Street. A soldier on horseback was dragged to the ground and beaten to death. The Lord Chief Justice of Ireland, Lord Kilwarden, had the misfortune of returning from dinner along Thomas Street in a carriage with his family. Reviled because of his propensity to prosecute rebels, he too was manhandled to the cobbles. In all his finery, he was piked and hacked to pieces, right before his daughter's eyes.

Please excuse my interruption, *Mammut*, but might I pose a question?

By all means, *Pterodactylus*.

While your narrative is certainly engaging and I am not by any stretch questioning its veracity, it occurs to me that you were not actually present for these events of which you seem to possess an intimate knowledge.

Ha, yes! I've been thinking that too! You can't get one past us birds, *M*.

I am not a bird, penguin.

You've got wings. That makes you a relative. Come on, *M*, 'fess up. You're nothing but a liar and exaggerator. Enough with the biased history lecture.

I beg your pardon, friends, but I know what happened during the failed rebellion because I overheard Anne Devlin discussing the events with her sister in the cottage. While I cannot verify the information through multiple sources – I am not a journalist for *The New York Times*, after all – Miss Devlin had no reason to lie.

She probably exaggerated, though. I lived in Boston. I know what the Irish are like.

That is not my place to say, *Palaeo*. I am merely conveying to you events as I understand them to have occurred. Does that satisfy your curiosity, *Pterodactylus*?

For the moment.

I'm sceptical of all this. I've got my beady real-bird's eye on you, *M*.

As I was about to say, Emmet tried to call off the uprising when he realised that his revolution was rapidly becoming a slaughter. It was too late. Fox's military, unsure of the magnitude of events, attacked the ranks of men massed in the street. Skirmishes stretched out into the night. By the end of it all, fifty rebels lay dead, alongside twenty British casualties. The insurgency had only lasted a few hours and ended in dismal failure.

To Sarah Curran's relief, Emmet emerged unscathed from the battle. He fled to a safe house in Harold's Cross, where he was housed as a lodger under the assumed name of Robert Hewitt. The other rebel leaders, Thomas Russell and James Hope, also went into hiding. Russell was sequestered elsewhere in Dublin, while Hope returned north, where he continued to evade the authorities until his death, forty-four years later.

Dublin was a dangerous place to live in the days subsequent to the rebellion. British troops raided the houses of any and all republican sympathisers. The very next morning, the soldiers paid a visit to the cottage in Butterfield Lane, where I was housed. Miss Devlin had only just applied a bandage to Miss O'Neill's injured head when the redcoats were spotted marching with intent along the street. Anne Devlin ushered Caoimhe out the back of the house, where she stumbled away and hid in the neighbour's privy.

Miss Devlin's eight-year-old sister was visiting to assist with the dressing of wounds. The evidence of their labours lay everywhere about the property. There was no concealing their involvement. The yeomen, when they burst in, showed no pity. The Devlins were beaten and arrested, even the child. Anne was conveyed to Dublin Castle, where she was to be interrogated by Henry Charles Sirr, the town major. Sirr was chief of police in the city and arch nemesis of Sarah Curran's father.

The crates containing my remains were left untouched by the British. There followed a period of many months in which I was ignorant of events that transpired. No-one came to the cottage until later that year, once winter held Dublin firmly in its grip. When finally I had a visitor, it was Caoimhe O'Neill, recovered from her injuries and sporting a scar at her temple. It was only then that I learnt the sorry fate of the various players in the 1803 Irish rebellion.

Hold on, *Mammut*. Is this going to be another one of your sad endings?

I am afraid so, *T. bataar*. Perhaps you should cover your ears.

If I could do that, I would have done it long ago, buddy. I'm just saying, what with the pterodactyl's reports on Nazi torture techniques and your habit of finishing stories with death and destruction, this whole tale you're spinning is enough to make a tyrannosaur dive headfirst into the nearest tar pit.

What can I say? The lives of hominids are replete with tragedy.

Are they, though? Back in Boston, all anyone wanted to do was have a good time. And it's not like their lives were brimming with joy.

You are correct, *Palaeo*. For a story to be successful, tragedy must be tempered with comedy. No-one is miserable all the time.

Right, and if you include a few laughs, it renders the sad moments all the more poignant. That's your working-class Bostonian in a nutshell, my friend.

And the Irish too, generally speaking.

Same difference, *M*. And yet so many books and movies portray ordinary working Joe and Jill Hominid as venal, humourless scumbags. What's with that? I lived in a bar most of my life. Down-on-their-luck bipeds aren't like that at all. Humour's all the poor have to get them through the hard times.

Nevertheless, *Palaeo*, there are certain unpleasant facts in my story that are inescapable.

I know, I know. Me and *T* just want to remind you that there's only so much misery we can take before we tune out.

I shall endeavour to make the narration more light-hearted, listeners, once we reach the next section of the story. Before you ask, *T. bataar*, the answer is soon, soon.

Neither you, *Pterodactylus*, nor you, *Palaeo*, were present at the very beginning of my narrative, when I explained to *T. bataar* how, when a member of the Clovis tribe of hominids was at my mercy, I ended his suffering swiftly, rather than resort to torture.

In my experience, bipeds have no such compunction. The yeomen of Major Sirr in Dublin Castle tortured Anne Devlin, who was only twenty-three years old at the time. With apologies to the squeamish fossils among you, she was kept naked in fetid conditions, repeatedly assaulted, and, when she still refused to inform on Robert Emmet, they half-hanged her.

This practice involves tightening a rope around the victim's neck until they lose consciousness due to strangulation. Prior to death, the rope is loosened, and the victim is revived. Once they have caught their breath, the process is repeated.

Not many hominids can withstand such tribulation, but Anne Devlin steadfastly refused to talk. She spat in the faces of her tormentors.

Major Sirr offered her bribes instead, which she refused. He then had the rest of her family imprisoned and their holdings seized. Again, she kept silent. Unable to break the young woman, Sirr had her cast into a dungeon in Kilmainham Gaol. She spent three years in complete darkness in a tiny stone room, without even a bed to sleep on. Dr Edward Trevor, the medical inspector of the prison, abused her relentlessly. Trevor had Anne's nine-year-old brother, James, brought to her, when he was on the verge of death after contracting pneumonia from his own time in jail. The boy passed away in her arms.

When she was finally released in 1806, the rebellion was but a memory. Most who had fought in the uprising were dead, but Anne lived on for a further forty-five years. She was harassed by the authorities on a regular basis and died penniless in 1851. A memorial service is now held for her every year in Dublin.

As for Robert Emmet himself, he could have fled to France under his assumed name, but his insistence on paying Sarah Curran one last visit precipitated his downfall. He was captured on 25 August and held in the same prison as his co-conspirators, although not for long. Robert was tried for treason on 19 September.

Due to the intransigence of potentially damaging witnesses such as Anne Devlin, and the general tight-lipped loyalty of his fellow United Irishmen, the Crown had precious little evidence with which to prosecute the young revolutionary. In order to secure a favourable verdict, the British offered Emmet's defence lawyer, Leonard McNally, two hundred pounds and a guaranteed pension. McNally folded, but his assistant, Peter Burrowes, refused to be bought and fought the case valiantly.

It mattered not. The verdict was preordained. Robert Emmet was found guilty of high treason and sentenced to be publicly hanged, drawn and quartered in Thomas Street. As was the tradition by law, presiding judge Lord Norbury was compelled to grant the defendant a rebuttal to the sentence. Emmet's long speech, frequently interrupted by the judge, is a model of defiance.

I shall not quote the speech in its entirety, for fear of drawing ever more criticism of my tale, but it is worth citing some of Emmet's final words on the subject of his rebellion.

I appeal to the immaculate God – I swear by the Throne of Heaven, before which I must shortly appear – by the blood of the murdered patriots who have gone before me – that my conduct has been, through all this peril, and through all my purposes, governed only by the convictions which I have uttered, and by no other view than that of the emancipation of my country from the superinhuman oppression under which she has so long and too patiently travailed; and I confidently and assuredly hope that, wild and chimerical as it may appear, there is still union and strength in Ireland to accomplish this noblest enterprise.

And then, at the end, the words for which he is remembered.

I am going to my cold and silent grave; my lamp of life is nearly extinguished; my race is run; the grave opens to receive me, and I sink into its bosom. I have but one request to ask at my departure from this world; it is – the charity of its silence. Let no man write my epitaph; for as no man who knows my motives dare now vindicate them, let not prejudice or ignorance asperse them. Let them and me rest in obscurity and peace, and my name remain uninscribed, until other times and other men can do justice to my character. When my country takes her place among the nations of the earth, then, and not till then, let my epitaph be written. I have done.

Whoa there, Mr Snuffleupagus. I smell elephant dung.

You are truly a rude and tiresome little beast, *Palaeo*. I am beginning to understand Queen Hatshepsut's frustration with you.

Hey, don't shoot the messenger, big guy. All I'm saying is you just quoted Emmet's exact words from a trial that, by your own admission, you did not attend.

This is true, *Mammut*. I wish to believe you, but this feels increasingly like a bedtime story rather than a statement of fact.

Oh, *Pterodactylus*. I am disappointed. I expect this sort of foolish criticism from the penguin, but you mean to tell me that you did not have time to read documents while you were a prisoner of the Nazis?

I did, but only those that were within view. Did someone leave a book on Robert Emmet next to you? Please explain.

Yeah, did an intern at the auction house conveniently happen to scroll through Emmet's Wikipedia page for an assignment while you peered over her shoulder? Just admit you're full of it, *M*.

There are ways and means to know things that may not be apparent to fossils such as yourselves, penguin.

Don't patronise me, furball.

Am I not correct in this, *T. bataar*?

Gotta say, birdies, the Big M's on the money about this one. Look, it's like this—

We shall tell them in due course, *T. bataar*. In the meantime, I have a story to finish.

Although I was not there to witness the event personally, *Palaeo*, apparently a large crowd formed in Thomas Street the following day to witness the young revolutionary's execution. That so many hominids would gather for such an occurrence speaks volumes about their nature.

Robert Emmet was hanged by the neck until dead, and then beheaded. No family members came forward to claim his remains, for fear of reprisals from the British. He was supposed to be buried in the grounds of a hospital near Kilmainham Gaol, but his bones disappeared and were never recovered. They may have been spirited away by loyal United Irishmen and placed in his sister's grave, but the location of his final resting place is unknown.

Perhaps some idiot will find his bones in years to come, dig them up and sell them at auction to a ghoulish private collector.

No lesser poet than Percy Bysshe Shelley penned an ode to the insurrectionist titled 'On Robert Emmet's Grave'. Here is a brief excerpt.

> *No trump tells thy virtues – the grave where they rest*
> *With thy dust shall remain unpolluted by fame,*
> *Till thy foes, by the world and by fortune caressed,*
> *Shall pass like a mist from the light of thy name.*

Thomas Russell eluded capture for another few weeks but eventually he too was arrested. The same fate awaited him. He was transported to Downpatrick Gaol, hanged and beheaded on 21 October. For their participation in the uprising, another fifteen labourers and tradesmen were also hanged.

Which only leaves two participants unaccounted for: Caoimhe O'Neill and Sarah Curran.

Despite their knowledge of Emmet's links to Sarah, gleaned by reading his correspondence to her, the British did not arrest the young woman, as her fiancé feared they might. However, when her father learnt of their secret engagement, he disowned his daughter. Since most of her friends were dead or in prison, she became destitute and sought refuge with old companions in Cork. There she met and married Henry Sturgeon, a naval man who was soon after posted to Haiti. Sarah went with him and bore him a child, who died at one month of age. Weakened by the difficult birth, Sarah contracted tuberculosis. She died in 1808, aged twenty-six. Her wish was to be buried next to her younger sister, who perished after falling from a window when she was twelve, but her stubborn father refused permission. Instead, her remains were laid to rest in County Cork, her father's birthplace.

It is said she never recovered from the loss of Robert Emmet and wore his ring until her dying day. Thomas Moore wrote a ballad in her honour titled 'She is far from the land'.

Oh, I know this one. I heard it sung many times in the bar.

Perhaps you will be so kind as to give us a rendition in that case, *Palaeo*?

I will, just to show you that a fossil can only know what happens in their presence. I'm not making this up because it was sung, for want of a better word, right in front of me.

Yes, yes, I understand. Please proceed.

Don't rush me, *M*. I need to do my vocal exercises first. Okay, here goes.

She is far from the land where her young hero sleeps,
And lovers around her are sighing,
But coldly she turns from their gaze, and weeps,
For her heart in his grave is lying.

Very touching, *Palaeo*. A round of applause, please.

Thank you, I'm here all night. Sorry, did you not clap, *T*? Problem with your hands?

This from a bird whose wings can't even get him off the ice.

You may be gratified to learn, *Palaeo*, that a pub in Dublin bears Sarah Curran's name. A tragic end to the romance of the young lovers, and the hopes of an uplifting revolution to free millions of Irish from servitude cruelly dashed. My initial excitement at being involved, in my own small way, was sorely tempered at the loss of so many promising young hominids. Ireland would remain under the yoke of the British for another hundred years and, even then, parts of it still are to this day.

It is fortunate for me that Caoimhe O'Neill was not arrested or killed during the struggle. My bones might otherwise have lain in that damp cottage for years, only to be thrown into a bog or gnawed by curs, perhaps even boiled up into a broth to feed the starving.

Instead, Caoimhe returned, still clinging to her plan to transport me back to America and sell me for profit. Whatever funds she and her brother might raise would line their own pockets. There was no longer any cause to finance.

After checking that I was still intact and had not been

plundered by the dragoons, Caoimhe promised to return. She had preparations to make for our departure to the United States, most of which had to be done in secret. There was a price on Caoimhe O'Neill's head, and informants were everywhere. She cut her hair short and resorted to dressing as a man in order to evade detection. There was a risk involved in visiting the cottage, but spies were less vigilant during the atrocious winter that soon enveloped Irish shores.

Wind rattled the shutters. Rain pelted the roof incessantly. Several leaks formed in the thatch, drip-dripping throughout the night. At one point, it rained for nine days straight. Without a fire in the grate, the cottage became shrouded in a damp mist that hung in the air and settled on everything, me included. What a wretched place that country is for weather. Any lyrical notions potential visitors to Ireland harbour are soon punctured by the harsh reality of constant precipitation. Give me the freezing steppe any day. It may have been cold, but at least it wasn't like standing under a showerhead all the lifelong day.

Caoimhe appeared again one rainy afternoon, accompanied by four men. Three of them began securing my crates and packing up the possessions of Robert Emmet and Anne Devlin. The other man, a maudlin character in his late thirties, inspected my skull at Caoimhe's insistence. He turned out to be Thomas Addis Emmet, Robert's older brother. He was a lawyer, and had been living in Paris, where he had continued discussions with Napoleon regarding potential assistance for the rebels. The First Consul's prevarication on the subject had proved fatal for those involved in the uprising.

Despite his heavy involvement in the 1798 rebellion, there was not a current warrant out for the arrest of Thomas Emmet, so he was able to travel freely. Now his brother was gone, and the revolution crushed, he had returned briefly to Ireland to pick up the pieces and prepare for his emigration to America. Caoimhe O'Neill and I were to accompany him.

'So, this is the creature you and Robert went to so much trouble to steal from the Americans,' Thomas said.

'I think of it more as an extended loan,' Caoimhe said. 'I'll be giving it back.'

'And collecting a finder's fee in the process, no doubt.'

'Only enough to set Con and me up for a few years. We're not asking for much.'

'It's worth a lot to those who covet such artefacts?'

'Plenty. Con's in Pittsburgh now, so I'll be meeting up with him there. He's trying to line up some buyers.'

Thomas Emmet ran his thick fingers along one of my tusks, as hominids are wont to do.

'We could have done with the money last winter,' he said.

'That's what I kept telling everyone, but you know Robbie. Once he gets an idea in his head, that's all he can think about.'

Caoimhe clicked her tongue as she realised she was referring to Robert Emmet in the present tense, as if he were about to walk in the door any minute and place his coat on the hook.

'You think he rushed into it, Caoimhe?'

'He did, Tom. I told him to wait until we sold this prize. Con and I were going to buy some crates of rifles and smuggle them back here. It might have been a different story if we'd had a properly armed militia, instead of a bunch of drunken scuts with pikes.'

'The benefit of hindsight,' Thomas said, sighing. 'No point in continuing the struggle now. It'll be years before we can raise enough support to mount another coup. The French are backing away. Napoleon's interests lie elsewhere. People are afraid. No, Caoimhe, I think it's time we left this place for good to seek our respective fortunes in the Americas.' He glanced around the damp cottage. 'This will always be with us, I suppose. Not easy to forget.'

'The stain of being Irish,' Caoimhe said. 'At least in the United States we can reinvent ourselves. Become something else.'

'Americans,' Thomas said. 'We will be Americans.'

With that, a lid was placed on the crate containing my head and I was plunged into darkness for another few months. An ocean voyage ensued, followed by a brief period in a dockside warehouse. From there, I was loaded onto a wagon and another journey began.

The issues I'm having with your narrative are multiplying by the minute, *M*, but there's one thing in particular that strikes me as odd just now. Maybe it's because I lived over a bar, but have you not heard it said that the story of the Irish is the story of alcohol? There's not nearly enough boozing in this tale.

While it is possible the two are intrinsically linked, *Palaeo*, such a general pronouncement is, at its heart, dismissive and bordering on racist. In my experience, the Irish are not the nation of drunks they are frequently made out to be.

There's a huge difference between being a drunk and being capable of drinking, *M*.

It is true, the Irish have a tolerance for alcohol that allows them to imbibe vast quantities of liquor while still functioning to the fullest extent of their capabilities. They can, I have observed, still drive a wagon and operate heavy machinery. Useful skills, when transporting several crates of mammoth bones across the hostile and forbidding territory that lies betwixt the port of Baltimore and Fayette County in the state of Kentucky.

Bit of a bumpy journey, was it?

Not one I wish to repeat anytime soon, *Palaeo*. Although my time concealed within the Guinness brewery in Dublin proved educational, I did not expect to have the lid of my packing chest prised open within the walls of another establishment dedicated to the craft of producing intoxicants upon arrival at our destination in America.

Ah, this sounds more like the Irish I know! Dive in, *M*.

'Oh ho,' proclaimed the gnarled individual holding the crowbar. 'Would you look at that, now? That's a beauty. The real deal.'

The bewhiskered hominid turned to Caoimhe, who loomed from the shadows to peer into the crate. She gave my skull the once-over, to ensure no damage had occurred during transit.

'Told you,' she said to the man, whom I deduced to be her older brother Conchobhar.

He rubbed his dirty palms together in glee. 'You've done well, junior. I didn't realise the specimen was so well preserved.'

'Cleaned up by its former owner,' Caoimhe told him. 'It's completely intact. Some of the joints are plaster, painted to look like bone, but, unless you're an expert, I doubt you'd be able to tell the difference.'

Conchobhar O'Neill was on the cusp of turning fifty and possessed the mien of a ruddy outdoorsman who had spent years sleeping under a blanket by a fire in the woods. His face was etched with the scars of hard living. As if to press this point home, he took a swig from a bottle of whiskey, which he then passed to his little sister. She eyed the bottle with suspicion, sniffed at it, and wiped the neck on her tunic before cautiously swallowing some of the liquid herself. She clacked her tongue and considered the taste before taking a second draw.

'What do you think?' Conchobhar asked. 'It's one of the new blends I've been working on.'

'Is it meant to taste smoky?'

'Aye. It was an accident, really. We had a wee conflagration in the storehouse and some of the barrels was charred. I used them anyway, for we was short. Lo and behold, the batch that come out had a rich, smoky flavour. I'm quite partial to it, myself, but it's probably an acquired taste.'

'One that's rapidly acquired,' Caoimhe said, taking another slug. 'That's a quare tipple, Con. Keep experimenting and we won't need to sell mammoth bones to get rich.'

'Listen, I told the preacher you was bringing rare trophies we could mount on the walls to give the place a wee bit of atmosphere.'

'We could do that,' Caoimhe said. 'Shouldn't be hard to hang the skull and tusks up over the tasting room. That way if any parties are interested in purchasing the beast, we can strike a deal over a glass or three of your firewater.'

'That's what I was thinking. Get them in their cups and drive up the price.'

'This is what I've been wanting to do this past year now,' Caoimhe said. 'Except them fools back home couldn't see the sense in it. Too busy working theyselves up over the redcoat occupation.'

'Aye, well, they're a bunch of bastards, right enough, but sometimes you just have to say feck it and move on. There's coin to be made out here, sister. The revolution's over and the Americans is building a new empire, one where there's a place for us.'

'Music to my ears, brother Con. When do we start?'

The whiskey of which the O'Neills were partaking is now commonly known as bourbon, for I found myself transported across land and sea to the distillery of the Reverend Elijah Craig, in Kentucky. Conchobhar had made his way there from Pittsburgh in an effort to elude authorities. There was a price on his head in the state of Ohio, and so he fled south, to wilder country, where lawmen feared to tread.

He found employment as a distiller with Elijah Craig, although he was also fond of the preacher's sermons. Craig was a Baptist who believed in religious freedom and economic opportunity. He had come south in 1782 and founded the town of Lebanon, which was later renamed Georgetown. Once established, the canny entrepreneur opened facilities for the production of cloth, paper, rope, lumber and whiskey. He even ran a school, which offered to teach Latin, Greek and science to its students. Fees were paid half in cash, half in produce. Room and board for a prospective scholar cost six pounds a year, or three pounds and five hundred weight of pork.

This was a time of great experimentation in whiskey. Small-batch farmers in Fayette and Bourbon counties were tinkering with the formula for producing spirits and coming up with groundbreaking results. They created a distinct identity for American grain alcohol production that would endure for centuries.

Conchobhar O'Neill's arrival in Kentucky came at an opportune moment. He quickly made himself a valuable asset in Craig's distillery, with his knowledge of whiskey-making techniques gleaned from the old world. Genuine Scots or Irish whiskey experience was highly prized in Kentucky at that time. For those who could be persuaded to make the journey, a profitable career beckoned.

The preacher was delighted to mount my head in the assembly hall of the distillery. This served not only as a tasting room for those wishing to purchase charred oak barrels of aged whiskey, but also as a place where religious services could be held. The reverend had no issue in reconciling the sale and consumption of alcohol with spreading the word of their Lord. Honestly, it seemed to make sense. The services I witnessed were imbibed with joy and good humour. Perhaps more hominids would turn to religion if inebriants were not only sanctioned, but also encouraged.

Conchobhar told Reverend Craig that his sister had also trained in the art of the still back in Ireland. This was not entirely true, but nor was it completely false. Caoimhe had spent enough time with her cousin Páraic on his farm in County Kerry, observing him brew up *poitín*, to possess a certain knowledge of the processes involved in distilling spirits. Convinced she would be a useful addition to the staff, Elijah Craig hired her on the spot. The fact she had spent time in France also enamoured her to him, for the whiskey-producing counties were named for Gilbert du Motier, le Marquis de Lafayette, from the royal House of Bourbon. Lafayette had fought against the British in the Revolutionary War and was a keen friend to Washington and Jefferson both.

Jeez, I hate to harp on but, again, how can you know this, *M*? Where even are you?

My skull was hanging on the wall, *Palaeo*. I have already told you this. Please try to pay attention.

Yeah, but still. I mean, I know the history of bourbon, obviously, since I spent most of my fossilife in a bar—

Then you will know how patrons talk. Please restrict your interruptions to considered objections only.

All right, all right. Keep going.

Caoimhe and Conchobhar huddled together on a pew in the assembly hall that first Sunday she arrived, listening to the preacher wax lyrical on the spiritual benefits of hard labour and the importance of showing kindness towards those toiling in the fields and factories.

'Not often you hear the boss evangelising to go easy on the workers,' Caoimhe whispered to her brother.

'He's an odd fish, sure enough,' Conchobhar admitted, scratching his scruffy beard. 'Not keen on the slavery either. A good cove, all round.'

'They're sweet on the French round these parts,' Caoimhe noted. 'Everything's got French names and your man there was pleased as punch I spoke some of the lingo.'

'Aye, you beguiled him with that, so you did. Listen, speaking of, did you hear the big fella Napoleon upped and sold Louisiana to the Americans?'

'So I understand. He needed money to fund his army. How much was he after getting for it again?'

'Fifty million francs, plus the cancellation of another eighteen million in debts. Comes to about fifteen million dollars, all up.'

'Jaysus. That'd keep you in clover for a while.'

'I know, madness, eh? The country's gone and doubled in size. They're just after conducting the final handover ceremony up in St Louis.'

'A lot of territory to control, of a sudden.'

'That's right. There's going to be disputes over boundaries, slaves, the fur trade and every other fecking thing. Reckon it'll be anarchy up in there for a while.'

'Land of opportunity, sounds like.'

'Could be.' Conchobhar nodded, exposing a row of rotten teeth as he grinned. 'Thing is, Caoimhe, we'll have to go.'

'Where? Into the new territories?'

'Aye. I've had no luck drumming up interest in your mammoth bones. It's a tricky proposition, for yer man Peale that you pinched them from has a reward out for their safe return. There's only so many fellers of means interested in such a prize, so it's going to be hard selling them without getting pinched ourselves. Having said that, I heard tell of a certain Captain Meriwether Lewis about to set out from St Louis on an expedition to the Pacific coast.'

'That's a long way, ain't it?'

'It surely is. He'll be gone a couple of year. Lewis is close with Jefferson, who wants him to map and explore the newly acquired lands, as well as forge a trade route across the continent. Also, he's to inform the natives who's in charge.'

'I'm sure they'll appreciate that.'

'Wouldn't want to be the one to break the news to the Shawnee, or any other myriad clans out there.'

'What's this got to do with us?'

'Well, he's to be on the lookout for mammoth bones and all. His attempts at securing a specimen from the salt lick down the way there have come to naught. Too many middlemen trying to turn some coin on the deal. Way I figure, if we was to front up at his fort in St Louis with the offer of a complete skeleton, cleaned and presentable like, maybes we could sell it to him for a good price without too many questions being asked as to its provenance. It'll be in the presidential mansion afore anyone realises they're the missing Peale bones everyone's after.'

'By that time, we'll be long gone. Disappeared into the new territory with enough gold to start our own town.'

'Exactly. O'Neillsville, maybes.'

'We can work on the name. How far is it from here to St Louis?'

'Three or four hundred mile. We'd need to be setting out soon, if we're to catch the captain afore he departs on his expedition.'

'Can we reach it by wagon? These bones are powerful difficult to transport, Con. It near killed me getting them this far.'

'If we had time, we could maybes go by water. Take a barge down the Ohio then turn up the Missouri. I reckon it's best we travel light. Take two horses and ride on up there in a week, ten days at most.'

'No bones, though?'

'You've got your sketches, haven't you? We should take a sample too. One of those big teeth, maybes. Yer man Lewis knows what he's looking for.'

'Leave the skull here, then?'

'Sure, he looks like he's enjoying himself up there on the wall. Probably listening to our every word. If we make the sale, Lewis can send a party down here to collect the crates. Won't be our problem no more.'

'I've sort of gotten used to having him around, the big fella. He's seen a lot these past few years.'

'Choose the biggest grinder in his gob, Caoimhe, and prise it out. We want to be impressing the good captain.'

'Hush, the preacher's after wanting us to join him in a wee prayer.'

'Be sure to ask Him Above for his blessing in our venture.'

'I've no doubt He'll be with us every step of the way.'

Do you mind if I interject, *M*?

Not at all, *Palaeo*. You appear to be the only one still listening anyway.

Your friend *T* has been asleep for the past forty minutes.

I thought he was rather quiet.

It takes some doing, putting an already dead fossil to sleep. But you managed it, *M*.

Where is *Pterodactylus antiquus*? Is she still with us?

The biped security guard took her into his office.

What's he doing in there?

There was a flash before, so I think he's taking photographs of the exhibits. Probably for his Facebook.

I hope he doesn't drop anything. What time is it, *Palaeo*?

It's late. Well after midnight. The auction starts at nine in the morning. It's going to be a long day, *M*.

Yes. There are three hundred and forty-five lots to get through, after all. I do hope we find good homes, *Palaeo*. You at least have enjoyed the constant company of bipeds since your disinterment. I have not always been so fortunate.

Spent some time alone, huh?

Far too long.

Figures. Never heard a fossil talk so much. I wouldn't worry, *M*. I'm sure you'll go to a nice natural history museum someplace, where there'll be plenty of other fossils you can bore with your fanciful tales. Me, I'd be happy to live the quiet life for a while, in the private collection of some rich hominid.

I thought you wanted to go back to a bar.

All your talk of Guinness and whiskey has put me off. I'm officially on the wagon, friend. No more boozy saloons for me. I don't think I can stand to hear one more rambling, drunken anecdote without a point or a punchline.

You don't want me to finish my story? There is only a little remaining to tell.

That's okay, *M*, you go right ahead and talk. One more for the road.

Speaking of the road, Conchobhar sought and was granted leave from Reverend Craig's distillery, under the auspices of travelling to St Louis in order to negotiate with a new client for a large order of whiskey. Caoimhe was to accompany her brother so she might gain experience in the business. Conchobhar also mentioned that she was adept at driving up prices, so Craig, ever the businessman, was happy for her to go along. They saddled an *Equus* apiece and set off on the road to Lexington.

The woodlands of Kentucky are majestic in the springtime. The days were warm, and the sky was clear at night. Caoimhe and her brother hunted game and cooked what they shot over a campfire every evening. This was a lifestyle Conchobhar had become accustomed to since leaving Ireland, but for Caoimhe this was all new, and it took her a few days to truly comprehend that she was free, the mistress of her own destiny.

'I should have come out to join you years ago,' she told Conchobhar as they supped on rabbit stew. 'Ireland's so restrictive. You can't do this, and you can't do that; everyone's always giving you orders and the fecking English won't leave us the feck alone. Whereas here? My God, it's an endless realm of possibility, Con. You can do and be whatever you like.'

'Welcome to my world, sister. It's an Arcadia all right, for the moment at least. I'm sure eventually the ways of the aul world will catch up with us and then all this majesty will be ruined the way it is back home. People – that's the problem, Caoimhe. You can't trust them to do the right thing by nature or each other. Take this purchase of the territories, for instance. You think these woods will still be standing twenty years from now? Probably not, I'd say. They'll all be chopped down to build cabins or the lumber will be sold for some nefarious business purpose. All the critters that live here will be gone, run off. Instead, there'll be people, more people. Towns will spring up. Schools and churches for all the infernal breeders to huddle together, so they can plot to rape the land, to steal it from them ones that lives here now. What must they think to see thousands of white ants swarming over their demesne, destroying everything in their path? Honestly, anyone who gets an arrer in their neck can't complain.'

'Have you encountered many Irish out here, Con?'

'Oh aye, after the rebellion in ninety-eight, you'd bump into a fair number of Celts who'd left the aul homeland seeking new pastures and a fresh start. Sure, you know yourself, Caoimhe, that the Irish condition is a dichotomy of restlessness and fidelity. You'll always love the aul country, and yet you'll always hate it a wee bit too. You want to be home, but you want to leave. We Irish are natural explorers, yet we carry our nationhood with us. Jaysus, we'd be the finest colonists in the world, if we could get our act together. Can't see that happening, though.'

'No.' Caoimhe laughed and passed her brother one of the bottles of smoky whiskey they had brought along to bolster their spirits on cold nights. 'At best, I can see us opening taverns everywhere, but that's about it.'

'Spreading the good cheer, aye,' Conchobhar said, taking a deep draught of whiskey.

'Here's to Ireland quietly conquering the world with her

saloons,' Caoimhe said, taking the bottle back and raising it triumphantly over the fire.

Hold on a minute, *M*.

What ails you now, *Palaeo*?

You're making all of this up, aren't you?

Indeed, I am not. As well you know I have excellent verbatim recall of conversations held in my vicinity.

That's just it, big fella. You weren't there when any of this happened. You just said the Irish lit out on horses. No mention of you packed into crates and loaded onto a wagon train. Remember? You're still in the assembly hall of the distillery, hanging on the wall. You didn't experience any of this. Caught you out, haven't I?

You have not, for I was there.

Oh, changing your story now, are you? How convenient.

No change to the tale, *Palaeo*. I was there, by the campfire, in a satchel hanging from Caoimhe's belt. Or at least part of me was. One of my molars. Still missing, incidentally, though I know where it is.

You had full awareness from a single tooth, *M*? I don't understand.

Neither do I, really. But that was the case, yes. You have always remained whole, have you not? Encased in rock? For many fossils, this is not so. Wherever my bones go, I go. If one of my vertebrae were to be posted to Australia, then I would be in Australia, while also being here.

That makes no sense whatsoever.

Agreed, but there it is. Recall the experience of your friend Queen Hatshepsut, for example.

She's not my friend.

Nevertheless, she is only with us as a severed hand, and yet she is able to converse. At the same time, she is aware of the rest of her body undergoing study in an Egyptian laboratory.

This science is so squirrelly, *M.*

You will get no argument from me on that front.

You can still feel your absent tooth? Where is it?

At the bottom of a river in Missouri. It has been there for two hundred and three years. I check in once in a while, but I try not to think about it too often. Not much happening down there.

You're never getting that back, huh?

No, but it was worth losing it to discover the fate of Caoimhe and Conchobhar O'Neill. Are you content for me to continue now, *Palaeo?*

Fine, but I have to admit, I'm suspicious regarding the veracity of this chestnut.

The O'Neill party did not make great haste in their efforts to reach Captain Lewis prior to his departure into the interior. Conchobhar was keen to arrive in St Louis, but the beauty of the countryside did not lend itself to proceeding on their mission at full gallop. Without any opportunity to secure fresh horses, the brother and sister rode at a steady pace.

Taking in the glory of nature and not exhausting their mounts was all very well, but by the time they reached Camp Dubois, just north of St Louis, Meriwether Lewis and William Clark were gone.

Camp Dubois was a frontier military fort that had been constructed by Second Lieutenant Clark the previous year, with the express purpose of housing and training the Corps of Discovery, the group of volunteer soldiers who would be tasked with sallying forth into the unexplored western territories.

A civilian trader visiting the camp was not unusual, though they did not get many women. Caoimhe had long since abandoned her male disguise. Once she left Ireland, there was no further need for concealment. Her cropped hair had grown back to shoulder length over recent months and, although she still wore the more practical britches favoured by male hominids, there was no doubting that Caoimhe O'Neill was of the female persuasion. All eyes turned on her when she and her sibling rode into the fort.

'I don't like the looks of this,' Conchobhar said as they tied up their horses.

'I can take care of myself,' Caoimhe said, staring accusingly at the gawking soldiers.

'Not that,' her brother said. 'Most of the garrison is missing. Unless they're out on manoeuvres somewhere, we might be too late.'

The stablehand told them that Sergeant Proctor was currently in command, which reinforced Conchobhar's fears. They reported to his office.

Proctor was a young non-commissioned officer with a stocky build and an elaborate moustache. He welcomed the new arrivals in a cordial fashion. The desk he had inherited from the previous commander was a mess of papers and unopened mail.

195

'Captain Lewis you're after, is it? Sorry, folks. He hasn't been here for a while. He went down to St Louis last week to finalise preparations.'

'Damn it,' Conchobhar said. 'Though it's not far. Maybes we can still catch him.'

'I doubt it,' Proctor said, eyeing Caoimhe up and down. 'Lieutenant Clark left six days ago with the bulk of the expeditionary force. My understanding is that the captain was to rendezvous with them at St Charles. That's a day or two upriver from here, depending on the speed of your vessel.'

'If we rode hard, do you reckon we could intercept the captain there?'

Proctor shook his head. 'I'm afraid not, Mr and Mrs O'Neill. They were intending to spend four or five days in St Charles prior to continuing the journey, but they'll surely be on their way to La Charette by now. That's the last white settlement on the river. Beyond that, it's wilderness.'

'We're siblings, not a couple,' Caoimhe told him.

'Duly noted,' the sergeant said, puffing out his chest a little at the news. 'Though it might be wiser to keep up a subterfuge while in camp, Miss O'Neill. I wouldn't want any of the men getting funny ideas. The presence of a woman can be disruptive in these remote outposts.'

'She's disruptive, all right,' Conchobhar said. 'I'd be for locking her in the stockade, I was you.'

'If you're staying, you can have my quarters, miss,' Proctor said. 'I'll bunk with the enlisted men. It's what I'm used to anyway. This expedition to the coast is all fine and dandy, but

I wish they'd send me a replacement officer.' Proctor shuffled a pile of documents on his desk. 'I can't make head nor tail of all this paperwork. A desk is not my natural element.'

'If you're offering us hospitality for the night,' Caoimhe said, 'perhaps I can assist you with some of that in return.'

Proctor's eyes bulged. 'Would you? I'd be most grateful. My reading skills aren't the finest. It's a mite embarrassing.'

'I'd be happy to help.'

'Only the one night, though,' Conchobhar said. 'If we're to stand any chance of conversing with Captain Lewis, we'd need to set out first thing in the morning.'

'I can provide you with a fast canoe,' Proctor offered. 'If you travel light and both take to the paddle, you'll gain ground on them. They're a big party, and they proceed at a snail's pace. You'll catch up, eventually. Do you have an important message for the captain?'

'Just a wee proposition that might save him some time and effort,' Conchobhar said, unwilling to divulge too much.

'Well, he's not expected back for two years – if he comes back at all – so he'll be mighty glad to entertain any notion that renders the trip shorter, I'm sure.'

'Listen, Sergeant,' Conchobhar said, draping an arm around the young man's shoulders. 'You seem like a fine fellow. If you're happy to house them, we'll leave our horses with you until our return, but I've a proposal for you in addition to that. Tell me, are you a whiskey-drinking man?'

'I have been known to partake on occasion,' Proctor said, his cheeks flushing. 'Never while on duty, of course.'

'Of course. Although you are in charge around here now, are you not?'

'That's true.'

Conchobhar produced a bottle of the smoky concoction from his satchel. 'Well, sir, wrap your lips around some of this and tell me what you think. I've a dozen bottles in them saddlebags out there. It's the latest thing, from down County Bourbon way. I promise you'll never think of whiskey the same way again.'

There followed a night of prodigious drinking, involving Conchobhar O'Neill, Sergeant James Proctor, a corporal by the name of Hugh Fields and, once she had made a dent in the sergeant's paperwork, Caoimhe herself. She wisely refrained from mingling with the soldiery, although several keen individuals found excuses to knock on the door of the sergeant's private quarters in order to convey some trivial message, just so they could get a look at her.

How creepy are hominid males? Seen that shit a million times in the bar. Some unsuspecting female having a drink after a long day in the corporate mines, sitting there, minding her own business when some leering male sidles up and tries to convince her to procreate in the bathroom. What's wrong with these hominids?

Many things, *Palaeo*. Many things, indeed. Penguins mate for life, do they not?

Fuck, no. Well, some do. The stupid ones. But the sex life of penguins is generally way more messed up than hominid researchers are letting on. Take my descendants, the Adélie penguins. *Pygoscelis adeliae*. They're into necrophilia, gang rape and polygamy. If a couple don't have enough pebbles for their nest, the male pimps the female out for stones. They cheat on each other; they divorce, reconcile and kidnap chicks if they can't produce one of their own. Penguins are the worst.

They must have inherited these deplorable traits from someone.

Don't look at me. I spent most of the last ten million years encased in ice.

As you well know from your years over the bar in Boston, *Palaeo*, the Herculean consumption of alcohol is usually followed by a gargantuan hangover the next morning. So it was for Sergeant Proctor and his aide-de-camp Fields. The O'Neills proved remarkably fresh, although Conchobhar confessed quietly to his sister that he was still inebriated, and that she would have to steer their pirogue out onto the river.

A long dugout canoe was thus provided for the Irish visitors. In exchange for the remainder of the whiskey – which Conchobhar swore off forever at a quarter past seven that morning – the pirogue was loaded with enough food and supplies to last a week. It was felt this would be all the time needed to catch up to Captain Lewis and his expedition to the interior. If required, the O'Neills could take on additional supplies at St Charles, or ask the poor wretches of La Charette for some milk and eggs.

Proctor pinched the bridge of his nose as he waved farewell to the Irish *voyageurs*. Caoimhe, seated at the rear of the canoe, steered them out into the middle of the river, while her brother groaned by the prow, dry heaving over the side.

'Are you about finished?' Caoimhe asked. 'It ain't easy going against this current. I could do with a hand here.'

'I'm sick, leave me alone,' Conchobhar told her.

'So am I. But if you don't start paddling, we'll never catch the Americans.'

'All right,' Conchobhar grumbled, leaning over the side to dunk his head in the river. He came back up in a spray of water, eyes wide. 'Jaysus! That's fierce cold, so it is. Don't be falling in, sister.'

'I'm trying not to. Quit rocking the boat,' Caoimhe said, reaching forward to bat at him with the paddle.

Shocked back to life, Conchobhar took up the oar and began stroking the water. Soon, they had developed a satisfying rhythm and made progress upriver, away from Camp Dubois.

A gentle breeze blew at their backs from the east, aiding the task. Grey clouds formed overhead, suggesting rain later in the day. The siblings fell into silence as they nursed their hangovers. By mid morning, they passed an island to starboard, opposite the mouth of a creek. Conchobhar cleared his throat, spat in the river and raised his paddle to rest for a moment. Caoimhe kept her oar in the water to hold them on station.

'Regretting giving away all that whiskey, now,' he said.

'Not three hours ago you swore never to touch another drop,' Caoimhe reminded him.

'Sobriety ain't all it's cracked up to be. Hair of the dog would go down nicely right about now. My head's pounding. All this fresh air's bad for you.'

'I've been doing the lion's share of work back here,' Caoimhe told him. 'I'm pulling us into shore on that wee island for a bit, so we can change places.'

'I'm after needing the privy and all,' Conchobhar said. 'Come on, then, let's have a break and stretch our legs.'

Taking to the paddle once more, the siblings steered the canoe towards the mid-river island and beached on a sandy margin. Conchobhar leapt from the bow and dragged the pirogue up out of the water.

'Back in a minute,' he said, hurrying off into the thicket to relieve himself. Caoimhe, for her part, got out of the canoe and rolled the cricks from her aching shoulders. They had some bread and nuts among the provisions, so she dug them out for a late breakfast.

There were signs of recent activity on the small island. Drag marks on the sand and footprints leading away into the bracken. The trail was faint, almost extinguished by the weather. Caoimhe pointed it out to her brother when he returned.

'Probably Lewis and his party camped here for the night,' Conchobhar said, kneeling to examine the tracks. 'Lot of moccasin prints, all different sizes. We're about five mile upriver from Camp Dubois, and Proctor said they didn't set out till late in the afternoon, so they wouldn't have gone much farther than this afore nightfall.'

Caoimhe handed her brother some grub. 'I'm going to explore for a bit and take care of my business.'

'I'll wait here,' Conchobhar replied. 'Don't be long and watch out for serpents. Whack them with a stick, if you see one.'

Caoimhe forced her way through the scrub, following the direction of the faded prints. The trail led her up an incline and into a wooded area, which provided shelter from the winds that whipped along the surface of the river. A dark patch on the earth indicated that a fire had been lit there. She kicked at the ashes before retiring into the lee of a bush to drop her britches.

Once her *toilette* was complete, she looked around the clearing to check if the party had left anything behind. She found nothing and made her way back to the sandy shore. Conchobhar awaited her there. He was staring down the river.

'Look at that,' he pointed.

Dark shapes moved across the water, heading for the right bank. A family of beaver, seeking shelter before the rains.

The pair took to the canoe once more and shoved off into the current. Feeling slightly recovered from the excesses of the previous night, they made good progress upriver. At lunchtime, they stopped briefly at St Charles, a small settlement that had hosted the expeditionary party for five days while awaiting the overland arrival of Captain Lewis.

William Clark had befriended several of the French families in St Charles during his brief time there, and was spoken highly of by a certain François Duquette, with whom he had dined. Duquette was more than happy to bestow the Irish travellers with as much information as he could in regard to his recent visitors, especially when Conchobhar informed him Caoimhe had recently returned from France.

Over a luncheon of cheeses and meats, Caoimhe regaled their hosts with tales from her time in Paris. They were astonished that she had mingled in such high society and were impressed by her meeting Georges Cuvier and Bernardin de Saint-Pierre. Duquette practically pleaded with the siblings to stay for a night or two, but they were forced to curtail their sojourn in order to resume their pursuit of the captain. Caoimhe promised they would return on their way back downriver, once the mission was complete.

Suitably bolstered by a sturdy repast, the O'Neills forged a path up the Missouri. They kept going until early evening, when, somewhat exhausted by their enthusiastic first-day efforts, they drew their pirogue into shore, tied off and made camp for the night in a copse of trees.

Despite the day's labours, Caoimhe was obviously enjoying the excursion into the wilderness with her brother. It was precisely what she had dreamt of doing as a child, when he would regale her with tales of the American hinterland. 'They seemed like friendly folk,' Caoimhe commented as she warmed her hands by the fire.

'Who, the Frenchies?' Conchobhar said, munching on a salted biscuit. 'Having you along on this trip certainly helps, sister. You've a way of charming the Continentals. I haven't always been so inclined, myself. Although they've been useful allies to us back home, there's no denying that.'

'I'd say there's a chance I'd have gone over there to live after the rebellion, if I didn't have you, Con. I'm not one for their airs and graces, but I likely could have secured myself a feller with some prospects or gone into business myself.'

'I'm certain you'd have prospered, Caoimhe, but what sort of business would ye have started? We've never had much capacity for that sort of thing. The O'Neills have always been independent operators.'

'Did you not run a courier service in Pittsburgh for a while, Con?'

'I did, aye, but it was a pain in the aul hole. Always some bastard ready to rip you off or steal the eyes out of your head. I'd to hire a bunch of gnarly-looking fellers armed with shotguns to protect the shipments. Cost me an arm and a leg. Weren't worth the trouble, in the end.'

'What's a shotgun?' Caoimhe asked.

'That's a Kentucky term for a long barrel smoothbore fowling piece that fires buckshot. Same as the blunderbuss your postman carries to protect the mail coach from highwaymen and brigands and such.'

'That'd be more effective than yon rifle of yours, then, wouldn't it?'

Conchobhar hefted his musket and checked the barrel was clean. 'At close range, aye, it would surely. Take your fecking head off. Not much use for hunting game, though.'

'You ever seen one of them grizzled bears, Con?'

'Heard of 'em. Huge beast, they say. Fearsome creature. Takes a dozen balls to bring him down. Suppose the good captain and his party might be running into a griz or three on dark nights out in the wilds.'

'There's none round here, though,' Caoimhe said, trying not to appear apprehensive as she squinted into the shadows.

'Don't think so. Your grizzer stays away from people, generally. Though you never know, maybes if word gets around there's a tasty Irish blade with French manners wandering the woods, they might be tempted to come down from the mountains for a looksee.'

'Fortunately, the smell of you will put them off.'

'That's not fair, now. Sure, I had a bath last week.'

'And when did you last wash that jerkin? Never, I wager.'

'Washing would only ruin it,' Conchobhar said. 'Look, if it gets cold the night, don't be sidling up to me for warmth, if it bothers ye so much.'

'I'll be fine,' Caoimhe told him. 'I can take care of myself.'

'So I notice. Taught ye well, I did. Chip off the aul block.'

'Aye, thank God for you, Con.'

'No need for that. I done my best, you know, with Da not being around.'

'You weren't around that much either. Always off gallivanting. Should have taken me with you years ago.'

'Aye, maybes. Shite flies high when it's hit with a stick, though, Caoimhe.'

'What, you didn't want me getting ideas? There weren't exactly ideas to be had back there. I always knew I didn't belong. I couldn't wait to get out.'

'I'm just saying, girl, you want to watch yourself with your French ways and all this talk of starting up in business. The higher the monkey climbs the tree, the further up its airse you see.'

'Don't worry your head, brother. I'm not about to become

some kept courtesan in a fancy frock. When I say business, I'm talking more in the nature of arms dealing or the smuggling of contraband. That'd be in the O'Neill line, would it not?'

'I'd say so,' Conchobhar said, filling his pipe with tobacco. 'Well, if that's what you're proposing, maybes we could talk further on the subject when we get back to Kentucky. If we secure this deal with yer man Lewis for the bones, it might be prudent to invest some of the gold in munitions and travel betwixt here and Europe, selling our guns to the highest bidder, eh?'

'Make use of my contacts in France and yours over here.'

'Now you're talking. Aye, well, let's catch up to the captain and conduct the transaction. We'll be rich in no time, girl!'

'Point that thing away from me, will you?' Caoimhe said, waving a hand to dispel the noxious smoke from her brother's pipe.

The night passed peacefully, with the embers of the fire keeping the siblings toasty warm until the pre-dawn. Despite the ominous clouds, it did not rain. The duo awoke to find themselves coated in a film of dew, but their spirits were soon lifted by coffee boiled over the freshly stoked fire and a boiled egg apiece. The sun had hardly broken the horizon when they set out in their pirogue, sculling their way upriver once more.

You know, *M*, I think this is your best work yet.

I don't follow, *Palaeo.*

No, you wouldn't. What I'm saying is this tale of the Irish siblings is damn fine storytelling. I'm pretty confident none of it's true but, hey, I'm past that now. Whatever. I'm enjoying the story for what it is.

I can assure you this is an accurate account of proceedings.

Sticking to your guns, eh? That's fine. I'm sure you believe it. You spin a good yarn, *M*. Thing is, in my experience with the hominids, I've noticed they're much more likely to believe something if it's conveyed to them in an authoritative voice. That's why they're so frequently sucked in by politicians. These guys make promises, talk a big game and the schlub voters say, 'Gee, sounds good!' and vote against their own interests. Politics 101. Make the masses believe you by acting confident and you can sell them a lemon.

Yes, I have to concur on this point, *Palaeo*. Hominids tend to overlook the truth because they are too lazy to bother seeking it themselves. They prefer to be told what to do and what to think. A fatal flaw in their character, which will forever hold them back from reaching their true potential.

You're just as bad, *M*. Never let the facts get in the way of a good story, eh?

History is written by the survivors, *Palaeo*. That is my final word on the subject.

It was late morning when the siblings came around a bend in the Missouri that revealed a small settlement on the right bank. The village only comprised a few meagre cabins. Pale smoke rose from a chimney. Two children hauled a sledge of chopped wood along a muddy trail, while a rugged man observed the approaching canoe. Despite the chill of the day, he was shirtless, with an axe rested over one shoulder. His bare chest bore a tangle of grey hair. He raised a hand in greeting. The O'Neills paddled in towards the shoreline.

'*Bon matang*,' he said in heavily accented French.

Caoimhe conversed with the man, although she had some difficulties understanding his Québécois argot. She translated for her brother.

'He says this is La Charette, the last outpost of whites on the river. He'd offer us something to eat but they don't have much, looks like. They're dirt poor and only just hanging on here.'

'I can see that,' Conchobhar said. 'Tell him it's all right, that we have sufficient provisions.'

Caoimhe conveyed her sibling's polite refusal of hospitality. The man seemed relieved.

'He wants to know where we're headed,' Caoimhe said. 'Says there's nothing out there but death and loneliness.'

'Quite the poet, yer man. Ask him when Lewis and his party passed by.'

The man nodded at the mention of the captain's name and spoke in his distinctive twang to Caoimhe.

'About three days back,' she told Conchobhar. 'We're making good ground on them.'

'Let's not tarry and bother him anymore,' Conchobhar said.

The man spoke again, peering into the bottom of their canoe as he did so.

'He says he hopes we have plenty of ammunition,' Caoimhe said, frowning as she struggled to translate. 'Uh, something about the Osage being on the warpath, I think.'

'Understood.' Conchobhar nodded. 'I don't think we'll be going that far into the territory. We'll catch up with the big feller, complete the deal and head straight back this way without delay. Tell yer man there we'll see him again in a week.'

Caoimhe passed on their thanks for the information and they pushed away from the riverbank into the stream. The man watched them go, waving farewell.

'*Ne purday pas vot kweer shevluh!*' he shouted, returning to the task of chopping logs.

'What did he say?' Conchobhar asked.

'Don't lose your scalp,' Caoimhe replied. 'Queer aul accent on him, that one.'

The fact of passing definitively into the unknown unsettled Conchobhar. He took to nervously scanning the trees that lined the shore. After navigating through a series of sandbars, they stopped for lunch mid-river, dragging the canoe up onto one of the sandy islands. Conchobhar fiddled with his rifle and ensured his sister's pistol was primed and loaded.

'I thought you said we'd be safe unless we forged deeper into Louisiana,' Caoimhe said, munching on a piece of cheese.

'You know how to use this, don't you?' Conchobhar asked.

'Some of us actually participated in the rebellion,' she told him.

'I would've, if I'd been there,' Conchobhar said. 'You ever kill a man, though?'

Caoimhe looked up sharply at her brother. 'That's not a thing to ask lightly.'

'Well, have you?'

Caoimhe stared out over the river. 'One feller for sure, and another that probably died from his wounds, though I can't be certain.'

'English?' Conchobhar asked, a little surprised.

Caoimhe nodded. She kept eating her cheese.

'During the uprising, was it?'

'No. Couple of redcoats scunnered with drink thought they'd take advantage of my charms one night after they stumbled out of the pub.' She threw the cheese rind into the water. 'Didn't go the way they thought.'

Conchobhar's countenance soured. 'Hope ye slit the throats on the both of them, Caoimhe.'

Caoimhe removed a short knife from the scabbard on her belt and turned it around to hand it to her brother. He took it by the handle and held it up to the light.

'You gave me that, 'member?' Caoimhe said.

'Aye. When I come back that time in ninety-six. This what you used on them?'

'It was,' Caoimhe said, taking the proffered dagger back. 'Stabbed them about a dozen times apiece. Lost my mind when I was doing it, but they never pinned it on me.'

'Sorry that happened to ye, sister,' Conchobhar said. He fondled his beard for a moment. 'You were right, you know. I should've spirited you away from there, instead of leaving you to the wolves. I didn't think this life was for you, but now I see I was wrong about that. I should've known. You're an O'Neill, through and through. Nothing less than a life of rampage will satisfy ye.'

'Aye, well.' Caoimhe sighed. 'We're together now, and that's all that matters. The past is behind and can't hurt us no more. No sense dwelling on aul wounds and slights.'

'That's the Irish way, though.'

'Didn't you say we were Americans now?'

Her brother laughed and bit into an apple. As they were finishing lunch and packing up the pirogue, a raft made up of two canoes lashed together appeared upriver. It was loaded with furs and pelts. Two men stood astride the raft, one at each end. Both held long poles. A third man paddled a single canoe alongside. Their beards were long and ragged. They had evidently been in the wilderness for many months.

'Trappers,' Conchobhar said, cradling his rifle. 'Be on your guard, Caoimhe. These sorts of fellers can be touched in the head from being out too long. Is your powder dry?'

'It is,' Caoimhe said, climbing into the pirogue while her brother stood his ground by the back of the boat, ready to leap in at a moment's notice.

The raft slowed as it entered the sandbars, the man at the prow carefully navigating a path so their precious cargo would not become stuck.

'*Français ou anglais?*' the man in the single canoe called out.

'Irish,' Conchobhar answered.

'*Parlez-vous anglais?*' Caoimhe asked.

'Yes,' the canoeist said. 'I do, but not my friends.'

'Hell of a swag you've got there,' Conchobhar said. 'I'd say you must be the finest hunters in these parts.'

'Something like this,' he said. He had halted his pirogue by a sandbar twenty feet away, while his companions held their raft on station a little behind. All three men eyed the O'Neills warily.

'Your intention is to do some trapping yourself?' the canoeist said. 'The game is good.' His command of English was excellent, his accent barely noticeable.

Conchobhar shook his head. 'Official business on behalf of the president. Can't say no more than that.'

'Something to do with the party we passed yesterday?'

'Could be.'

The canoeist spat in the water. 'We were told this was American territory now, is that so?'

'Sold by Napoleon for about the price of all them pelts.'

The canoeist translated this for his companions. They snorted in disdain.

'This is not a fair exchange,' the Frenchman said.

'Take it up with your glorious leader,' Conchobhar replied.

'We wish to take it up with you, *mon ami*. As *citoyens* of *la France*, we demand additional compensation.'

'Here it comes,' Conchobhar said. 'As if you greedy bastards don't have enough coin lashed to your boat, there.'

'You misunderstand me, monsieur,' the canoeist said. 'We are not interested in money.' He waved his hand dismissively. 'We have plenty of this. I think your wife should stay with us for a few days, until your return. It is not safe for a woman in this locality.'

'*Je ne suis pas sa femme, je suis sa soeur,*' Caoimhe said.

'His sister!' the Frenchman said, while the others laughed.

'And she speaks French? Even better. In this case you will have no problem, monsieur.'

'Best you move along, now,' Conchobhar said. 'Once you sell those pelts in St Louis, you'll have enough money to pay for six months in the whorehouse.'

'I am afraid I must insist,' the canoeist said, cocking his rifle. 'Now, if the lady would step out of *le pirogue*, I will come over to—'

The trapper never got to complete his sentence. Caoimhe shot him in the chest with her pistol, which she had been concealing in her lap. He fell backwards out of his pirogue onto the sandbar, tipping the canoe in the process. Conchobhar fired a follow-up shot at the two men on the barge, who both ducked out of sight behind the pile of furs. He pushed the canoe into the water and jumped into the back. As Caoimhe scrabbled for powder, Conchobhar paddled hard upriver, past the lashed-together canoes. Although she had not finished reloading, Caoimhe levelled her pistol at the raft to ensure the two men kept their heads down.

Once they were past the barge, Caoimhe loaded a ball into the barrel of the pistol. Since they were unable to turn their heavily laden raft against the current, the Frenchmen did not set out immediately in pursuit. Instead, one of them jumped down into the water to check on his companion, while the other produced a long-barrelled rifle, resting it on a pile of animal pelts as he lined up his shot.

'Con!' Caoimhe shouted. 'Stay down!'

Conchobhar paddled grimly, trying to put as much distance

between them and the trappers as possible. Caoimhe aimed her pistol back towards the raft. She fired at the same moment as the French rifleman.

'Missed,' she said. 'Should I reload or take to the paddle?'

Conchobhar slumped forward in the canoe, paddle slipping from his hands into the water. Caoimhe made a grab for it but was too late. The oar was carried away downriver by the current. She threw her arms around her brother and propped him up. His eyes bulged. Her hands felt a wet patch on his back.

Conchobhar had been shot through the base of his right shoulderblade, shattering the bone. The ball was lodged in his chest cavity. He drew in a rasping breath of air.

'Get us away,' he moaned. 'Don't stop.'

With no time to waste and the current already reversing their gains, Caoimhe laid her brother down in the back of the boat and took up her paddle, furiously striking the water to pilot the canoe out of range of the shooter on the barge. She headed for the cover of the embankment, which was shrouded in a tangle of tree roots. When finally she chanced a look back, she saw the trappers were occupied taking care of their own injured man. If he was dead, she had no way of knowing.

Conchobhar had passed out but was still breathing. The manner in which he lay sprawled in the rear of the canoe, a pool of blood forming under him, filled Caoimhe with fear. Her mind raced as she tried to calculate how long it would be before they caught up to the expeditionary party, especially if she were the only one paddling.

Caoimhe sculled for an hour, until she was certain she had

time to stop and tend to her brother's wound. She steered the canoe into the shallows and tied it off to a protruding root. After rummaging in her knapsack for a moment, she produced a small flask, opened it and took a slug.

'I've been holding out on you, Con,' she said, 'but given the circumstances ...'

Caoimhe raised her brother's head and tipped whiskey between his parted lips. He coughed, spluttered and came to. There was blood in his spit.

'Did we get away?' he said, his voice husky.

'For the moment. No idea if they're at our heels.'

'Why'd you stop, then?'

'To see to you.'

'Where'd you get that whiskey?'

'Never you mind. Lean forward so's I can get a look at the wound.'

'You'll have to help me.'

Caoimhe assisted her brother in sitting up. He slumped forward into her arms with the effort.

'Jaysus, I'm numb all over,' he said, and she could hear the fear in his voice.

Caoimhe tried her best to clean the bullet hole, but it was a mess. She tore off a piece of her sleeve, cleaned it in the water and placed it over the gouge in an attempt to stop the bleeding. When she looked her brother in the face again, he was pale.

'Can you hold on till we reach Lewis and them ones? They'll have a surgeon with them for sure.'

Conchobhar grinned. There was blood on his teeth. 'I'm fecking done, sister. You best be leaving me here. They'll be after you, for sure. Catch you too, if you've to go on with all this extra weight in the boat.'

'Are you soft in the head? Where would I leave you – here on the riverbank?'

'Aye, with my rifle. I'll slow them up, give you time to reach Lewis. You can bring a doctor back with ye. I'll wait.'

'You will not, Conchobhar O'Neill. Sure, you can hardly hold your head up, never mind fire a rifle. We'll keep pressing forward.'

Conchobhar gripped his sister's wrist. 'I'm sorry it turned out like this, Caoimhe. I should've done things different.'

'Would've, should've, could've. Quiet now, Con. Rest up and I'll get us where we're going. Just hold on and you'll be a rich man the morrow.'

'Always the morrow,' Conchobhar said, smiling. He lay back in the canoe and closed his eyes.

Caoimhe crawled to the prow and took up her paddle. She untied the rope and steered the pirogue back out into the river.

The current was strong, making progress difficult. Caoimhe had to stay close to the banks and concentrate so she would not direct the boat into rocks or sandbars. It was brutal labour, and after an hour she was sweating and exhausted. She sculled to starboard until she reached a pebbled section of shore, where she could beach the canoe for some respite. She jumped out and dragged the boat up onto the shale.

Conchobhar seemed at peace, so she stooped by the water's

edge to fill her canteen. She drank thirstily and splashed some cold water over her face and neck. It was mid afternoon and the sun was shining down through the grey clouds, the light dancing on the surface of the river.

'Not a bad spot,' Caoimhe said. 'Like that place we went to down in Cork, 'member? You and cousin Páraic went fishing for salmon. They was swimming upriver to spawn and leaping out of the water like deer. Never ate so well in our lives, eh?'

Caoimhe rose and went to the boat, where she knelt and placed her hand around the back of Conchobhar's neck in order to administer some water from the canteen. His skin was cold and clammy. He did not respond to her touch.

Caoimhe rubbed his cold hands in hers and listened at her brother's chest, then at his lips to check his breathing.

She repeated these actions for ten minutes before resigning herself to the fact he was dead.

Caoimhe sat on the pebbles at the river's edge and stared out across the water. Whatever her thoughts were, she kept her own counsel. She remained in that position for an hour, perhaps more. She might well have sat there all night, had it not been for the sight of a canoe approaching from downriver.

'Ah, for fuck's sake,' Caoimhe said. 'Really? Have ye not hurt me enough?'

Two of the trappers were in the pirogue. Caoimhe could not tell from such a distance if one of them was the man she had shot. They were making good speed.

Knowing that a gun battle was only likely at close quarters, Caoimhe shoved the canoe back into the water and jumped in.

She turned about and set to paddling hard, away from the men stalking her.

It only took a few minutes for her to realise that her boat was too heavy, and the combined strength of two men paddling behind meant they would overtake her before the hour was out. She had no time for such luxuries as sentimentality or mourning.

'I'm sorry, Con,' she said to her brother's corpse. 'I know you'd want me to do this, even though it's a terrible sin.'

Caoimhe rolled Conchobhar's body up and over the side of the pirogue. He slipped under the water for a moment, and then resurfaced. Buoyed by the current, he floated downriver towards the approaching trappers. They paused for a few seconds as they worked out what was happening. Now they knew her brother was gone, they redoubled their efforts in pursuit, confident they would catch their prey without further interference.

Lacking time to think, Caoimhe moved to the rear of the boat and began paddling again. The canoe sliced through the water with ease now. She glanced back occasionally, to confirm the trappers were still following. They were not making ground as quickly as before, but still had an advantage over her. Slowly, the distance between the two canoes was closing.

Rough water indicated a set of rapids lay ahead, as the river funnelled through a small ravine. Caoimhe dug into her final reserves of strength to push the canoe through the channel against the current. Once she was clear, she turned sharply so the pirogue came in behind a large boulder, where it lodged momentarily.

Caoimhe loaded her pistol and her brother's rifle and laid them either side of her thighs in the canoe. She waited in the shadow of the rock, shivering, paddle at the ready, until she could hear French voices.

'*Tu la vois?*'

'*Pas encore. Fonce, fonce!*'

As the Frenchmen's canoe entered the canyon, Caoimhe pushed against the boulder with her paddle and steered her pirogue out into the fast stream. The current caught her boat and whipped it around. The small vessel gained speed and zipped between the rocks, heading straight for the hunters.

When they saw her coming, they dropped their paddles and fumbled for their weapons. The loss of momentum caused their boat to lurch sideways and almost capsize. It spun back towards the mouth of the canyon.

Caoimhe set her own paddle down and took up the arms, pistol in her right hand, heavy rifle held shakily in her left. As her boat passed that of the Frenchmen, she fired both weapons at point-blank range.

The man sitting in the prow of the boat was hit in the face by the ball from her pistol. His mandible was blown off in a pop of red mist and he fell back into the water, dead.

The rifle shot hit the other man in the belly. He grunted and slumped forward in the canoe.

The two boats knocked against each other as they were spat out of the fast water. Caoimhe's canoe spun as she set down the rifle and began to reload the pistol. She watched the other pirogue as it drifted away, and then veered closer.

The man inside was the one she had shot downriver. He was still alive, even now. He moaned and turned over, and then sat up, blinking until he noticed Caoimhe fumbling with her pistol.

'*Putain de salope*,' he said. 'That's the second and last time you shoot me.'

He raised his rifle, aimed it at Caoimhe and rolled his neck. Her pistol was nowhere near ready to fire, so she dropped it, spat her contempt in the water and turned to meet her fate. She opened her arms wide and faced the French trapper down.

The man did not shoot. Although Caoimhe neither heard nor saw its flight, an arrow pierced the trapper's neck. He gurgled blood and dropped his rifle, which clattered over the side of the canoe into the river. He clawed at his throat in shock.

A second arrow appeared in the man's chest, then a third. He collapsed in the canoe, dead.

Caoimhe slowly turned, arms still raised, to look up at the embankment. Three tall men dressed only in loincloths, their bodies painted white, sat on horses surveying the scene with the sun at their backs. She awaited the thunk of an arrow in her own chest, but none came. One of the men pointed to a section of shore where she might beach the pirogue. Unable to quite believe what was happening, Caoimhe did as the men of Osage Nation bid her, for it was they who had saved her.

It had been a grim day and Caoimhe's nerves were frazzled. She paddled in and pulled the boat up onto the sand. At her wit's end, she stood with hands on hips, waiting as the three men rode down the declivity to the water's edge.

Two of them slipped from their mounts and, ignoring Caoimhe completely, rifled through the belongings in the pirogue. She watched as they collected the guns, ammunition and supplies, before loading them onto their horses.

The third man regarded her without any obvious emotion. Caoimhe stared back. After a moment's consideration, he spurred his horse towards her, circled around and leant down to offer his hand. Caoimhe grasped it and jumped up onto the horse, behind him. She placed her arms around his waist and held on as the horse clambered back up the muddy bank, the other two men following after on their own mounts.

Whoa, hold that *Equus*, *M*. I need a breather to process everything that's happened.

My apologies, *Palaeo*. I have been in full flow. The fateful journey of Caoimhe O'Neill is a lot to take in.

Good stuff, though. This is better than the movies. Hey, you know what you should do, *M*?

No, but I do enjoy others telling me what I should do.

Really?

Of course not.

Right. Still. I have an idea. It's a real money-spinner.

Inflict it upon me, if you must.

You should write up this entire tale as a series of ten forty-five-minute episodes and sell it to The History Channel as a show. No, wait, even better, you know those Netflix guys?

I do not.

Yes, you do, *M*. The ones who send DVDs out to customers in the mail.

Hmm. I may have seen one of their packages on an intern's desk. What of it?

Well, I overheard two of the hominid nerds saying that Netflix just announced they're moving into streaming content over the internet.

I have no idea what that means, *Palaeo*.

Geez, get with the times, *M*. It means the hominids will be watching movies and television shows online, like they do with YouTube.

Episodic internet television? My dear bird, that seems unlikely.

I'm telling you, man, it's the future! You should pitch them your show.

Yes, well, I shall speak to my agent. May I continue?

Season finale, let's go!

As the Osage rode off into the landscape, Caoimhe rested her cheek against the man's shoulder and wept for the loss of her brother. The rider's bare back was warm, and she held on to him as they passed over streams and hills, through forest and brush. As night began to fall, they reached a village, and were met by dozens of children who were curious to see what prizes had been plundered. They pointed and poked at Caoimhe as she passed. She did not react. She no longer knew how to feel. The only thing she was certain of now was that she was a long way from Ireland, and that she might never find her way back to so-called civilisation.

The rider shucked her off in front of a tent of women. They looked her up and down for a moment before ushering her inside. The teepee was warm and cosy, filled with blankets. Caoimhe was invited to sit and offered a bowl of food, which she ate as four women watched. She tried speaking English, but none of them understood. When she reverted to French, one of the older women nodded and replied in a basic manner.

'*Nous sommes Wazhazhe,*' she said.

Caoimhe would not understand until much later that this was how the Osage referred to themselves in their indigenous language, *Wazhazhe* meaning Mid-waters. They were also called *Ni-u-kon-ska*, or People of the Middle Waters.

In broken French, Caoimhe explained as best she could to the attentive women where she was from and what had happened to her. The old woman translated for the others. They expressed sorrow for the loss of her brother and admiration for her bravery against the French trappers on the river, men they had run afoul of before and did not appreciate one bit.

Caoimhe slept soundly that night, overcome with exhaustion and soothed by a shaggy dog that crept into the tent to sidle up to her for warmth. The women laughed at the sight of them intertwined in the morning, and Caoimhe came to understand through sign language that the dog had chosen to lie with her because she stank.

The women led her down to a creek, where, out of sight of the men, they stripped naked to bathe. Caoimhe undressed to join them. There was much mirth and interest in her pale skin, tanned only on the arms and neck. After washing, Caoimhe found that her clothes had been confiscated and, later, burnt. Only her satchel of personal effects was spared from the fire. She was given a buckskin dress and moccasin boots instead, which she found extremely freeing and comfortable.

The women of the Wazhazhe admired the new addition to their tribe. Any uncertainty Caoimhe harboured about what her role was to be was soon settled, as she was led back to the village and put to work preparing food and sewing. Since she had always been adept at both, her skills were welcomed. The praise and hospitality she experienced were unexpected. Caoimhe was treated as if she were the long-lost relative of a member of the tribe, finally come home.

Every time Caoimhe tried to converse with the French-speaking elder concerning their plans for her, the woman waved her away and told her not to worry. After a few days, the man who had brought her back came by to check on her. Caoimhe was presented to him with a certain pride, and he seemed to approve of her makeover. Sensing she might be lodging with the Wazhazhe for an extended period, Caoimhe had already made an effort to learn some basic words of their language. Thus, she was able, in a faltering way, to thank the man for his assistance on the river.

Although he raised his eyebrows and smirked at her efforts with their tongue, he nodded that he understood. The elder spoke to him then, and Caoimhe recognised enough of the words to comprehend that he was being informed she spoke English and French.

To her amazement, the man then spoke to Caoimhe for the first time.

'*Vous nous aidez*,' he said. You help us. It was more of a statement than a question.

Caoimhe agreed with gusto, realising she could be a valuable asset to the tribe in the coming negotiations when men like Captain Lewis appeared on the horizon, claiming the land was theirs.

Days passed into weeks, and Caoimhe adapted to her new way of life among the Wazhazhe. She learnt many things – that the sun was *Mi*, the water was *Ni*, a man was *Nikka*, a woman *Wak'o*, and their god, who was neither male nor female, was called *Wah-kon-tah*.

Although she was kept busy in the village and did not object to her many labours, during moments of reflection Caoimhe was acutely aware that any chance of catching up to Lewis and Clark had long lapsed. The notion of persuading Lewis to purchase my bones – which remained in Kentucky – now seemed fantastical. In truth, as time passed, Caoimhe lost interest in the idea altogether and was only reminded of it when she looked through her satchel of trinkets and found my molar.

She showed it to the elder woman, who nodded, claiming it could be the tooth of Honga, the great earth spirit. The sketches Caoimhe had once made of my form would have proven useful, but they had long since been destroyed. I was being forgotten.

Summer came to a glorious end and was followed by autumn and then winter. Caoimhe fell under the romantic attentions of the man who had rescued her from the river, a development she did not find unwelcome. They were bonded together by the start of spring. Caoimhe now spoke in the Wazhazhe language and was considered a full member of the tribe. She could be seen, on occasion, sitting by the edge of the creek, staring into the distance, perhaps thinking of Ireland and France and Conchobhar.

There was no way of Caoimhe knowing that after his triumphant and somewhat unexpected return to St Louis in 1806, Captain Meriwether Lewis was appointed by President Jefferson as superintendent of Indian affairs for the territory of Missouri and surrounding region. Although his expedition had not experienced serious conflict with the Osage Nation during their time travelling to and from the west coast, Lewis predicted it was only a matter of time before the United States would engage in open war with the tribe.

Rather than submit to their new masters, the Osage Nation carried out a series of raids on European settlements. The effrontery. With vast sums of money to be made in the fur trade, Lewis decided it was prudent to drive the Osage from their lands, rather than risk a downturn in business. Not wishing to engage their own military in a protracted and dangerous campaign, Lewis simply armed rival tribes, such as the Potawatomi, Sac and Fox. With modern weapons at their disposal, their rivals decimated the Osage and forced them into an eventual treaty.

Caoimhe O'Neill was killed in September 1807 by a Potawatomi brave who shot her through the liver. She had been trying to defend the children of the village at the time, including her two-year-old daughter. Woman and child plunged together into the Little Osage River and were swept away by the current. The child drowned, unable to extricate herself from her mother's arms.

My tooth, which Caoimhe still had in the satchel about her waist, tumbled out when the drawstring came undone, and sank to the bottom of the river. It lies there still today, among the smooth pebbles, unseen and unknown, near the border with Kansas.

An awful lot of people die in your stories, *M*.

That's the hominids for you, *Palaeo*. They are such fragile little things. Their time in this world is but temporary. We must try not to become too attached to their ephemeral lives.

Have to say, I'm still suss on you experiencing all this through a molar. Seems a mighty convenient narrative device.

I too am sceptical.

Ah, hello again, *Pterodactylus*. We missed you.

Very kind of you to say, *Mammut*. While I was recently engaged in a conversation with my warthog friend, I caught the gist of your tale. It seems as if you are approaching the conclusion.

Indeed I am.

You know, this whole incident with the tooth explains a lot for me.

How so, *T. bataar*? You have been reflective of late. Lost in deep thought?

Something like that, bro. I'm glad you told this part of the story from the point of view of a tooth, and I totally believe every word.

I had no idea *Tyrannosaurus* were so gullible.

Mammut's right, penguin. What would you know? You've been frozen in rock for the entirety of your fossilife. Some of us haven't been so lucky. There's bits of me still buried in the sand of the Gobi Desert. And as for teeth? Don't get me started.

I did not wish to point this out before for fear of causing offence, *T. bataar*, but I noticed when we first met that you are missing several of your impressive incisors.

Thank you, *Mammut*. Such is the price of being a Lizard Hero. Everyone wants one of my gnashers as a souvenir. After the bipeds dug me up, four teeth were stolen during my first night above ground. Four! I know where each of them is now, because, as you say, I can feel them. I know everything that's going on around them. It's a huge bummer. I wish I had them back. It's like being in five places at once.

So, you're backing up this harebrained split-consciousness theory?

Totally! Let me just check in with my errant chompers. Let's see, yup, no change in circumstances, as far as I can tell. One of them is currently sitting in the window of a store called Wunderkammer in Melbourne, Australia. The joint sells scientific ephemera, artefacts and curiosities. For company, I have a Venus flytrap plant, a piece of amber full of ants, a sextant and a Bunsen burner. Conversation is limited, although the view is great. I get to watch the bipeds bustling back and forth along the street, and there's a courthouse across the road. Plus, the shop is on one of those Melbourne corners where they have hook turns, so I get to see car accidents all the time.

It's great. So many hominids getting smushed. Ah, the old Australian hook – so unnecessary, and the cause of so much delicious carnage! The prices in there are dubious, by the way. Seven hundred and fifty bucks for one of my teeth seems cheap. If I had the cash, I'd buy it myself, get it shipped back here and pop that pearly white back into place.

How did your tooth wind up there?

Well, how did we end up here, penguin? It's a long story, longer than *Mammut*'s. You guys really want to hear it?

No!

No, thank you.

I think I'll pass.

Anyhoo, tooth number two is also behind glass, in the Raffles Museum of Biodiversity Research in Singapore. It's not a bad life – a bit boring but I get plenty of attention. A kid tried to steal me once, but he didn't get far. I think he was flogged for his trouble. They don't fool around over there. Zero tolerance. They're especially harsh on dental-related crime.

Now, where's number three? Ah yes, lying in a Portuguese field. Just sitting there, enjoying the sunshine. Would you believe a balloonist dropped it? I suppose you'd have to, given everything else you've heard tonight. How did it come to be in the possession of a man in a hot air balloon, I hear you ask?

No-one's asking, *T*. It's fine to gloss over this one.

Whatevs. So that leaves fang four. That little feller is currently located in Russia. Kept in a velvet-lined box, in the private collection of an oligarch. He likes to show it off to the ladies at parties. He has a lot of parties. And a lot of ladies.

The sights I've witnessed through that tooth, oh boy. You want to talk about the mating rituals of hominids? I could tell you a few things that aren't in the textbooks. So yeah, *Mammut* speaks the truth. He can still feel that molar in the river. No doubting him on that front.

Thank you for your support, *T. bataar*. It is most appreciated.

All good, bro.

Huh. Well, hopefully that will never happen to *P-dac* or me. I don't like the sound of it.

You'll be fine. You're too small and puny to be sold as separate pieces.

I have a query for you, *Mammut*.

Yes, *Pterodactylus*?

What was happening to the rest of you while your tooth was paddling up the Missouri River?

I remained where the O'Neills had left me, in custody of the Reverend Elijah Craig, mounted on the distillery hall wall. News had reached the pastor of Conchobhar's demise, since his body had floated downriver and been recovered by the villagers at La Charette. When one of the trappers' corpses appeared a few days later riddled with arrows, it was assumed the Osage Nation had claimed the lives of both parties. No-one had really gotten to know Caoimhe O'Neill, and so she was soon forgotten, written off as yet another victim of progress and encroachment. Her body was never found, not that anyone was looking. The O'Neill adventure in the Americas died with her.

How long did you stay mounted over the bar?

Quite some time, *Palaeo*. I was a popular feature in the distillery, a frequent topic of conversation. You must recall that the idea of behemoths walking American soil was still captivating to many at that time. There was much talk of my kind still existing out in the wilderness. Many a drunken hominid boasted of having glimpsed an American elephant from a distance, unable to get closer before we conveniently vanished into the woods. I may still have been there today, were it not for the intervention of a Shawnee tracker called Philippe Softshoe Jones. This biped had converted to Christianity. He came in to visit the distillery with a party of cavalrymen many months after the deaths of my Irish charges.

He knew you for what you were.

Indeed, *Palaeo*. I suppose he had heard stories, passed down through the generations among his people. He was not well pleased to see me reduced to a trophy on the wall of a glorified liquor store. He canvassed Reverend Craig on my behalf, beseeching him to release me from penury. The reverend was reluctant at first, but when Philippe told him that my display amounted to a vulgar insult to the heritage of the Shawnee, Elijah realised it might be prudent, for the sake of good relations, to hand me over to Mr Jones.

Thus, one bright spring morning in 1808, after years of listening to the inebriated conversations of frontiersmen heading for Louisiana to make their fortune killing animals and native peoples alike, the dusty crates containing my bones were retrieved from storage and united with my head. Philippe – who was a fine young man with his heart in the right place, even if he did condemn me to almost two centuries of loneliness – had me loaded in entirety onto the back of a wagon, which he personally drove into the wilds of Kentucky, following an ancient trail into the mountains known only to his people.

Back on the wagon, eh, *Mammut*? Where were you off to this time?

The Black Mountain mastodon graveyard, *T. bataar*. It was a place of which I was dimly aware. One hears stories of mass burial sites, where the ancients went to die. Perhaps I would have travelled there myself, all those thousands of years ago. Ironic that I should wind up there anyway, conveyed by a hominid wishing to honour the old ways.

It was no easy task for Philippe Softshoe Jones carrying me up the mountainside. He had to make many trips, for the path was faint and treacherous. *Ursus americanus* observed the young man's travails from behind a yellow birch but did not intervene, knowing the duty he performed was a sacred ritual. I am sure she hoped someone might do the same for her, when her time came.

He climbed up through the hardwood forest until he came to a cave, high on the mountain. Scattered inside were the dusty bones of those who came before me. They were tired old mastodons and bears, begrudgingly welcoming of the company, confused as to why I was only appearing now, over ten thousand years too late.

Philippe left me with them. He spent the night and departed in the morning, never to return. He had completed the task of honouring my remains. I thanked him for that, at first. Little could I know then that he would be the last hominid I would see for almost two hundred years. The other dead animals listened rapt to the tale of my exploits, just as you have so patiently these past hours, friends.

Not so patiently, when you think about it.

Not so rapt either, bud.

As months passed into years our conversation dwindled. There simply wasn't much to talk about anymore. Some of my companions in the cemetery stopped talking altogether until, eventually, mine was the only voice that echoed around the walls of the cave. Figuratively speaking, of course.

You bored them to death. No, *beyond* death. Quite a feat, *M*.

In 1896, fire swept through the forest, *Palaeo*. Loggers were the cause. In the conflagration, the mouth of the cave collapsed, and we were plunged into permanent night. No-one came to dig us out. The Shawnee were mostly gone by then anyway. It would not have been such a harsh sentence, was I truly kaput, but my spirit lived on. I was condemned to simply lie there, alive but not alive, permanently stuck between realms.

This awful condition of stasis continued throughout the twentieth century and beyond, until, one wondrous day not so very long ago, a metal claw opened up the side of the mountain. The hominids had returned and were shocked to discover a graveyard from a bygone age. The land was being developed, you see, the forest cleared to make room for a hillside casino resort.

For a while, I believed myself rescued. I thought I would be mounted on a wall again, or even made whole, as a visitor attraction. But no, the construction of a casino is an expensive endeavour and, in the eyes of those who dislodged me from my second grave, I was little more than money lying on the ground.

This is why I am here, with you. I am being sold to finance a gambling den.

Everything has a price, M. Even us.

I have spent so long in darkness, with no other company but my own. That is why I have talked so much tonight, my friends. I am sorry to have bothered you so. You must find me tedious, an old bore. It is good to finally hear the voices of other creatures, to no longer feel alone. I never expected to wander this earth again, even if only in spirit. But I am glad to have spent this brief time with you, *T. bataar*, and you, *Palaeo*, and you, *Pterodactylus*. It has been an honour getting to know you.

Are you going somewhere, M? You sound like you're about to jump off a building.

After tomorrow's auction, we will all be going elsewhere, *Palaeo*. Probably not together.

I hope I end up in the mansion of some rich playboy!

I am hoping for a quiet spot in a respected museum, among other flying reptiles.

I'll be content anywhere except over another frigging bar. What about you, M?

I would enjoy a window where I can look out and see mountains. Perhaps a river. A wide plain that freezes over in winter. A place where deer come out of the forest to forage for food. Somewhere I can rest in peace. Forgive me, I mean in pieces.

Was that your lame mastodon attempt at a joke?

Hey, let's not discourage him. Sure, it's a little obvious for my taste, but I'll take what I can get. This entire tale has been a veritable famine of LOLs. Really, *Mammut*, next time you tell this story, you need to inject some humour, bro.

Not too much, I think, *T. bataar*. No comedian ever won the Pulitzer. Besides, it is not my natural inclination.

Duh, we know. You lean towards the tragic, *Mammut*.

My apologies for that, but I am tired, friends. All I wish for is a return to the earth, to die, as I should have thirteen thousand years ago. I want to sleep, so I may dream of the steppe. Please, hominids, if you're listening out there, it is not much to ask. Let us sleep.

Epilogus hominum

On 25 March 2007, an auction was held at a rented showroom on Fifth Avenue and 29th Street in New York City. Three hundred and forty-five lots were up for grabs, including the sixty-seven-million-year-old skull of *Tyrannosaurus bataar*, the severed hand of an Egyptian mummy, the skulls of lions, hyenas and warthogs, a meteorite whose alleged origin was Mars, a ten-million-year-old penguin fossil, the skeleton of a pterodactyl, a seventy-five-thousand-year-old dire wolf skull, a sixty-two-ounce gold nugget from Western Australia and, last but not least, our mammoth narrator, who in reality was little more than a huge tusk.

Virtually all of the exhibits were on open display and available for inspection by potential buyers, as well as anyone else who happened to be wandering through. Once underway, bids came in not only from the floor, but also by phone and on eBay.

The hottest property was the skull of *T. bataar*. Two phone bidders went after it, driving up the price. It sold for $276,000 to a 'mystery buyer' from Los Angeles. That individual also spent $50,000 on the dire wolf skull.

The mystery buyer was actor Nicolas Cage. The other person bidding on the *T. bataar* skull turned out to be Leonardo DiCaprio, who had to make do with the skull of a mosasaur (*Platecarpus ictericus*) instead.

The mummy's hand sold for $4,500 to gallery owner Anders Karlsson, from Santa Monica. Karlsson is a regular at the IM Chait Natural History Auction, which the Beverly Hills business holds every year in Manhattan. It is a fun day out for collectors and dino-lovers, with every price range covered. The following year, for example, saw the skull of a unicorn dinosaur sell for $75,000 (it's a cousin to *Triceratops*), Miocene sharks' teeth fly out the door for a bargain basement $250 apiece, a gold nugget make someone happy for $145,000, and another mammoth tusk sell for a snip at $65,000. No word if he was a relation to our own humble *Mammut*.

IM Chait performs all necessary due diligence with its lots, doing everything in their power to verify provenance. Occasionally, some crafty operator manages to pull the wool over their eyes. Such was the case with *Tyrannosaurus bataar*, who as we know was illegally exported from Mongolia. *T. bataar* tells the story of how this happened better than I do, so if you've read this far you already know the sordid details. The United States Attorney's office in New York investigated on behalf of the Mongolian government and came down hard on the seller, Florida resident Eric Prokopi, who eventually served time for smuggling.

The Department of National Treasures – my apologies, the Department of Homeland Security – contacted Nicolas Cage in 2014 to alert him to the fact his dinosaur skull was stolen goods. Mr Cage graciously agreed to donate the skull back to its rightful owners, and it was repatriated to Mongolia in 2015. Its new home was to be the Central Museum of Mongolian Dinosaurs in Ulaanbaatar, which already housed an almost-complete *T. bataar* skeleton, also stolen by Eric Prokopi, also sold at auction (for $1.05 million) and also returned by the New York federal prosecutor. Reports from Ulaanbaatar are that our boy has settled in nicely and that his favourite movie is now *Con Air*.

Mr DiCaprio held on to his mosasaur skull for an even shorter space of time. In December 2008, he sold it to Russell Crowe. Ten years later, the skull featured as one of over two hundred lots in the auction Mr Crowe held to raise funds for his divorce from Danielle Spencer, alongside a chariot from *Gladiator* and the leather jockstrap he wore in *Cinderella Man*. In an interview with Channel 9's *Today* show, Crowe said he could not recall the exact details of how he came into possession of the mosasaur skull but that vodka had almost certainly played a part. The skull sold for $A65,000.

Comedian John Oliver purchased the jockstrap, as well as a jacket from *Les Misérables*, a set seat from *American Gangster* and a *Robin Hood* costume. He donated the items to the last remaining Blockbuster video store in Anchorage, Alaska, in order to help them drum up custom. Mr Crowe responded by donating the money raised for those items to the Australia Zoo Wildlife Hospital, which named a new facility in Mr Oliver's honour – the John Oliver Koala Chlamydia Ward. Mr Oliver briefly considered shutting down his show when he found out, claiming that the establishment of a koala chlamydia ward was an accomplishment that could never be surpassed.

For the most part, the hominids that appear in this story are actual historical personages. Where possible, *Mammut* seems to have remained faithful to events and even dialogue from the era. Georges Cuvier's views on race and catastrophism expounded herein, for example, are mirrored in his writings from the period.

Of the rest, Charles Willson Peale, Georges-Louis Leclerc, Rembrandt Peale, Moses Williams, Hatshepsut, Éleuthère Irénée du Pont, Bernardin de Saint-Pierre, Robert Emmet, Nicholas Cresswell, Arthur Guinness, Thomas Russell, James Hope, Sarah Curran, John Philpot Curran, Anne Devlin, Wolfram Sievers, Henry Charles Sirr, Michael Dwyer, Thomas Emmet and Elijah Craig were all real people. Details of the exhumation of the mastodon, its subsequent display in Philadelphia, the tour of France, the second Irish rebellion, and the early days of the Lewis and Clark expedition are reasonably well captured, albeit with *Mammut*'s customary hyperbole.

The beast's propensity for exaggeration and invention comes into play elsewhere in the narrative. Although we know megafauna was wiped out approximately ten thousand years ago due to the arrival of Clovis and the warming of the climate, there is no way of verifying *Mammut*'s specific story in this regard. We are obliged to take his word for it.

Similarly, the hand of the mummy sold to Anders Karlsson at auction has not been verified as that of Hatshepsut. One would hope that not to be the case, lest Mr Karlsson's progeny be cursed for generations.

Finally, to Conchobhar and Caoimhe O'Neill. Extensive research has revealed no record of their lives, so they may have sprung entirely from the narrator's imagination. That is not to say the O'Neill siblings did not exist. History often only records the lives of the wealthy and famous, so their exploits may have fallen through the cracks. These tricky names are pronounced *Kon-uh-kur* and *Kee-va*, by the way. Don't feel bad if you've been saying them wrong this whole time. Just don't do it again.

Incidentally, the O'Neill clan owns a large property down the road from my parents' house in County Antrim. It is situated by the edge of Lough Neagh and includes a derelict castle, said to be haunted by a banshee called Maeveen who has lived with the O'Neills for two thousand years. The O'Neills are descended from the first High King of Ireland, Niall Nolligach, or Niall of the Nine Hostages, so they've been around for a while. Despite living in the region for just as long, my family has no castle. They still rent.

Mammoth tusks have become a regular feature at auctions over the past decade. Several million of the creatures spent the last dozen millennia locked in the Siberian permafrost, which has recently begun to melt. It is legal to gather mammoth tusks as you would berries in Russia, provided you have a licence. This sudden proliferation of high-quality ivory has caused a shift in the market.

The sale of elephant ivory has been banned internationally since 1990, although that has not stopped poachers from killing up to 30,000 elephants a year to bolster the black-market trade of the product. Now that more and more mammoth tusks have become available, dealers are selling vast quantities of this legal ivory to international markets, particularly China, where an estimated one hundred tonnes a year of mammoth ivory are consumed by artisans who carve the material into jewellery and other trinkets.

While some see this as a sustainable alternative and a means to wean China off elephant ivory – the mammoths are already dead, after all, and their remains are literally lying around the tundra in Siberia – others feel the consumption of mammoth ivory only worsens the situation. The number of mammoths locked in the permafrost may be enormous, but they are a finite resource. In addition, the legal sale of mammoth ivory provides a useful cover for black marketeers looking to offload poached elephant tusks.

Recognising this problem, a number of American states – New Jersey, New York, California, Hawaii, Illinois, Nevada and New Hampshire – have expanded their ban on the sale of elephant ivory to include mammoth ivory. If you see it, don't buy it. *Mammut* and his still-living descendants will thank you.

Why is the permafrost melting in the first place? The absence of large animals roaming the old Mammoth Steppe has resulted in soft snow forming a layer of insulation on the soil. Previously, *Mammut* and his friends would have compacted the snow, allowing a deep cold to penetrate the earth and keep the steppe frozen. Without them, the rise in temperature has caused the release of carbon equivalent to what would be produced if all the world's forests were burnt two and a half times over.

The Harvard Woolly Mammoth Revival team, headed by Dr George Church, has proposed a radical solution to the permafrost thaw in Siberia. They want to resurrect the mammoth. They feel the restoration of a great herd could hold the key to combating climate change. Cloning the mammoth back to life is not currently feasible, although the Church Lab is hard at work on making it happen.

The intention is to use genome engineering to take DNA from mammoth genomes found in the well-preserved specimens now thawing out and place it into the cell cultures of living elephants. The Asian elephant is 99.96 per cent mammoth anyway, although that 0.04 per cent is crucial to get right, if a warm-weather animal is to be adapted for a cold climate.

Once perfected, an embryo can be generated in an artificial uterus and birthed. This has already been achieved with other animals, such as the mouse and sheep. Asian elephants will raise the first generation of mammoths. Once a large enough breeding population is established, the herd will be released in the Arctic. Dr Sergey Zimov and his son Nikita have already established one such suitable site. Sixteen square kilometres of land in Siberia are currently home to bison, moose, reindeer, musk ox and horses, recreating pre-Clovis steppe conditions. Dr Zimov hopes to add mammoth in his lifetime.

It is called Pleistocene Park.

But why am I telling you all this, when you can hear it direct from the mastodon's mouth?

Epilogus mammut

Time. Deep time. That is where we live. I used to count the years, tick them off on some cosmic calendar. A hundred. A thousand. Ten thousand. Now I understand that it doesn't really matter. Even when you think you're dead, you're not. We live forever.

Thirteen thousand, four hundred and fifty-one years have passed since the antediluvian days. The blink of an eye, for some. An eternity of torment, for others. I fall somewhere in between on that scale. The years of loneliness have evaporated, like mist burning off a lake in the morning sun. The fog has lifted. I can see all the way to the horizon.

I am alone no more. The great herd has been restored. Somehow, those bipeds I always resented for their wanton savagery found a way to undo their mistakes. They have wound back the clock, discovered a means of cheating oblivion. Annihilation has been averted. It didn't look good there, for a while, but when their backs were pressed so tightly against the wall they could taste their own farts, the hominids came through with the goods.

The world has not been fixed. It is still ailing from so many years of abuse. But it is getting better. On the mend. Sometimes you have to stare into the brink in order to understand how close to the edge you are standing, and how precipitous will be the fall.

We are helping, doing what we can, what we were born to do. This is the reason we exist, the reason we have always existed. Every party needs a cool head, someone who sees the big picture, a guest who can tap into deep time and explain that the future lies in our past. Need an answer to your dilemma? Look over your shoulder, friend. Everything that is happening now has happened before. And, to be quite frank, a mammoth problem requires a mammoth solution.

We number in the tens of thousands now. Our calves are born naturally. The hominids helped us with that, for a while, but we no longer need their science. New spirits are coming into the world, to join the old souls like me, who still hold those repositories of ancestral memory. My tales of Clovis, *Canis dirus* and the glacier regale the calves. They know we were extinguished and still survived. Most of them don't believe me when I tell the story, or perhaps they do when they are young. Once they reach maturity, they set aside childish fantasies of the old steppe. My stories are dismissed as fairytales, legends created to teach and entertain. I am one of the few who know the truth.

The steppe is different now. Smaller, but growing. It is a nature reserve, where hunting is not permitted. We are too valuable. That did not deter some dogged individuals from trying, some years back. Those fools. They thought it would be easy, coming in here with their rifles and jeeps. Only three of them made it out alive. Much to the bafflement of the hominids who monitor the park, the herd was protected by a pack of *Canis dirus*, who took great satisfaction in hunting the hunters.

Still today, the biped scientists argue over why wolves protected the mammoth young. If only they could hear, I would happily explain.

The agreement is back in place.

I negotiated a pact with the alpha not long after I found myself at the head of a herd, decades ago. He knew who I was. He turned out to be a cousin of my old, old friend. Deep time, playing its part again, throwing up an ancient bond too strong to be broken by the passing of a few miserly millennia.

For the first time, I overheard bipeds speculating that we might possess a means of interspecies communication. Not many subscribe to the theory, which sounds outlandish to most hominid ears. This amuses me. Really, humans? You're only working this out now? We were here long before you ever walked the steppe. Just because we never developed holograms or opposable thumbs doesn't mean we're stupid. Animals are just as clever as you. In some cases, more so. Most cases. All right, in pretty much every case. Think you're top of the food chain? We let you believe that. Your vanity knows no bounds and must be continually fed if we are to share this world. It is oh so tiresome humouring you.

Still. We appreciate you coming to an epiphany. Relentless growth is not sustainable. Everything has limits. It cannot have been easy for you to admit this and change your nature. I know not everyone has been on board with the new way of living. Some fought tooth and claw to preserve their self-appointed right to conquer and destroy everything in their path but, thankfully, common sense prevailed. I'll be honest – I was worried. I thought you'd lost sight of what is important in this world, that you had forgotten what a blessing it is to be granted even the briefest time walking the steppe.

We have another chance now. We know what is required. We know what we're doing, so don't worry, my puny two-legged friends. We'll take it from here.

I have to go soon. The herd is on the move. Each year that passes, winter is colder. This is good. This is the way it should be. I will lead the herd across the park, compressing the snow as we go, preventing trees from taking root. We will teach the calves the old ways, which are now the new ways. The only ways.

I have heard tell of another place, far to the south. I do not know exactly where it is. But I know it is hot and tropical. Rumours have come to me on the winds of great reptiles walking the earth once more, and flying on the warm currents, and swimming in the oceans. I hope it is true. I hope my friends are there. I miss them.

It is time to leave. Trunks are raised, calling me to the march. Breathe it in. Breathe in that cold air. Isn't it wonderful? It is *so* good to be alive. To be *Mammut*. To be home.

Acknowledgements

Thanks are due to several hominids who helped make this story possible. Eirian Chapman for her constant support (emotional, financial, illustrative, amorous). Brendan Fredericks for being a top-notch agent and publicist who has always championed my work and books in general. *Kocham cię, cipa.* My publisher, Aviva Tuffield, for her unparalleled contribution to Australian literature and instant enthusiasm for this left-field proposition. My editor, Felicity 'Thanos the Mad Titan' Dunning, for her finger snaps that made the universe a better place. Sonny Day and Biddy Maroney for transporting us to another world with the cover. Liz Gilbert, who has more love in that big old heart than anyone alive and is happy to share it around. Jo Duck for capturing my good side, or at least recognising there might be one. Clarion calls to Dave, Meg, Tom, Favel, Christos, Tony, Emily, George, Gilbert and all the lovely bipeds at the University of Queensland Press.

Thanks to the Native Languages of the Americas team for their assistance in checking the Wazhazhe language words.

A special mention to my two- and four-legged friends at RSPCA Victoria, Phillip Island & District Motorcycle Club, and Island Story Gatherers.

Bibliography

Crowgey, H. G. 2008, *Kentucky Bourbon: The early years of whiskeymaking*, University Press of Kentucky, Lexington.

Dugatkin, L. A. 2009, *Mr. Jefferson and the Giant Moose: Natural history in early America*, University of Chicago Press, Chicago.

Geoghegan, P. M. 2002, *Robert Emmet: A life*, McGill-Queen's University Press, Montreal.

Goodrick-Clarke, N. 1985, *The Occult Roots of Nazism: The Ariosophists of Austria and Germany, 1890–1935*, Aquarian Press, London.

Grann, D. 2017, *Killers of the Flower Moon: The Osage murders and the birth of the FBI*, Vintage Books, New York.

Haynes, G. (ed.) 2009, *American Megafaunal Extinctions at the End of the Pleistocene*, Vertebrate Paleobiology and Paleoanthropology, Springer, New York.

Huckelbridge, D. 2014, *Bourbon: A history of the American spirit*, William Morrow, New York.

Kurlander, E. 2017, *Hitler's Monsters: A supernatural history of the Third Reich*, Yale University Press, New Haven.

Leclerc, G. L. & Smellie, W. (translator) 1781, *Natural History, General and Particular, translated into English*, W. Strahan, T. Cadell & W. Creech, London.

Lee, S. B. 1833, *Memoirs of Baron Cuvier*, Harper, New York.

Lister, A. & Bahn, P. G. 2007, *Mammoths: Giants of the Ice Age*, University of California Press, Berkeley.

Martin, P. S. 2007, *Twilight of the Mammoths: Ice Age extinctions and the rewilding of America*, University of California Press, Berkeley.

Mezrich, B. 2017, *Woolly: The true story of the quest to revive one of history's most iconic extinct creatures*, Atria Books, New York.

Moulton, G. E. (ed.) 2004, *The Lewis and Clark Journals (Abridged Edition): An American epic of discovery*, 2nd edn, Bison Books, Winnipeg.

Richardson, E. P. 1983, *Charles Willson Peale and His World*, Harry N. Abrams, New York.

Rudwick, M. J. S. 1997, *Georges Cuvier, Fossil Bones, and Geographical Catastrophes: New translations and interpretations of the primary texts*, University of Chicago Press, Chicago.

Stanford, D. J. & Bradley B. A. 2013, *Across Atlantic Ice: The origin of America's Clovis culture*, University of California Press, Berkeley.

Stone, R. 2002, *Mammoth: The resurrection of an Ice Age giant*, Perseus Publishing, New York.

Ward, P. D. 1997, *The Call of Distant Mammoths: Why the Ice Age mammals disappeared*, Copernicus, Göttingen.